CITY OF ROCKS

OTHER FIVE STAR WESTERN TITLES BY MICHAEL ZIMMER:

Johnny Montana (2010)
Wild Side of the River (2011)
The Long Hitch (2011)

CITY OF ROCKS

A WESTERN STORY

MICHAEL ZIMMER

FIVE STAR
A part of Gale, Cengage Learning

GALE
CENGAGE Learning®

Detroit • New York • San Francisco • New Haven, Conn • Waterville, Maine • London

GALE
CENGAGE Learning·

Set in 11 pt. Plantin.

LIBRARY OF CONGRESS CATALOGING-IN-PUBLICATION DATA

Zimmer, Michael.
  City of rocks : a western story / by Michael Zimmer. — 1st ed.
     p. cm.
  ISBN-13: 978-1-4328-2557-7 (hardcover)
  ISBN-10: 1-4328-2557-7 (hardcover)
  I. Title.
PS3576.I467C58 2012
813'.54—dc23   2011036303

First Edition. First Printing: February 2012.
Published in 2012 in conjunction with Golden West Literary Agency.

Printed in the United States of America
1 2 3 4 5 6 7 16 15 14 13 12

For
Wayne and Yvonne
And peaches and jigsaw puzzles

FOREWORD
THE AMERICAN LEGENDS
COLLECTIONS

During the Great Depression of the 1930s, nearly one quarter of the American work force was unemployed. Facing the possibility of economic and government collapse, President Franklin Roosevelt initiated the New Deal program, a desperate bid to get the country back on its feet.

The largest of these programs was the Works Progress Administration (WPA), which focused primarily on manual labor with the construction of bridges, highways, schools, and parks across the country. But the WPA also included a provision for the nation's unemployed artists, called the Federal Arts Project, and within its umbrella, the Federal Writers Project (FWP). At its peak, the FWP put to work approximately six thousand five hundred men and women.

During the FWP's earliest years, the focus was on a series of state guidebooks, but, in the late 1930s, the project created what has been called a "hidden legacy" of America's past—more than ten thousand life stories gleaned from men and women across the nation.

Although these life histories, a part of the Folklore Project within the FWP, were meant to be published eventually in a series of anthologies, that goal was effectively halted by the United States' entry into World War II. Most of these histories are currently located within the Library of Congress in Washington, D.C.

As the Federal Writers Project was an arm of the larger Arts Project, so too was the Folklore Project a subsidiary of the FWP. An even lesser known branch of the Folklore Project was the American Legends Collection (ALC), created in 1936, and managed from 1936 to 1941 by a small staff from the University of Indiana. The ALC was officially closed in early 1942, another casualty of the war effort.

While the Folklore Project's goal was to capture everyday life in America, the ALC's purpose was the acquisition of as many "incidental" histories from our nation's past as possible. Unfortunately the bulk of the American Legends Collection was lost due to manpower shortages caused by the war.

The only remaining interviews known to exist from the ALC are those located within the A.C. Thorpe Papers at the Bryerton Library in Indiana. These are carbons only, as the original transcripts were turned in to the offices of the FWP in November, 1941.

Andrew Charles Thorpe was unique among those scribes put into employment by the FWP-ALC in that he recorded his interviews with an Edison Dictaphone. These discs, a precursor to the LP records of a later generation, were found sealed in a vault shortly after Thorpe's death in 2006. Of the eighty-some interviews discovered therein, most were conducted between the years 1936 and 1939. They offer an unparalleled view of both a time (1864 to 1912) and place (Florida to Nevada, Montana to Texas) within the United States' singular history.

The editor of this volume is grateful to the current executor of the A.C. Thorpe Estate for his assistance in reviewing these papers, and to the descendants of Mr. Thorpe for their co-operation in allowing these transcripts to be brought into public view.

An explanation should be made at this point that, although minor additions to the text were included to enhance its effect,

no facts were altered. Any mistakes or misrepresentations result-
ing from these changes are solely my own.

Leon Michaels

December 4, 2010

Just talk into this tube and it'll catch all my words, huh? All right, but I want to tell you up front that I'm not going to repeat the pack of lies that have been told about me in the past. I ain't no hero, and I never was called the Idaho Kid, like that Sacramento newspaper claimed last year. They came out here and took my picture and asked a bunch of questions, but what they printed afterward wasn't nothing like what I told them. So if that's what you're planning to do, you can just take your recording machine there and leave.

All right, I'll trust you that you'll copy this word for word, and help put a stop to the fabrications I keep hearing about that incident.

You asked me to tell my story from the beginning, but I'm not really sure where that is. I want you to know what happened, but I also want you to know why it happened. That's not as easy to put into words.

You know, a lot of people go to those moving-picture shows down at the Rialto or the Gaslight, and they think they're seeing the real McCoy as far as what it used to be like out here in the 1870s and 1880s, but that's not the way it was. The fact is, when it comes to the truth, those movie folks don't know squat. You take a guy like William S. Hart or Tom Mix, or that kid that was in *The Big Trail* . . . what's his name? John Wayne? They all try to come off rough-barked, but they're nothing but a bunch of lilies compared to men like Ian McCandles and Ben Ryder

11

and Yakima Tom Candy. Those boys, McCandles's gang, they're what the dictionary had in mind when it described rough-barked. McCandles's men would've ate those Hollywood cowboys for breakfast, and been hungry again before noon. I'll tell you something else I've noticed about those cowboy pictures. They're clean. Fancy boots and engraved Colts, and barely a smudge of dirt anywhere. What happened out there in City of Rocks wasn't clean. It was grimy and smelly and gut-numbingly cold. And it was scary. Men died for stupid reasons, and when they did, they didn't just grab their chests and fall over. They got knocked down hard and the life spilled out of them like blood from a butchered hog.

I guess I ought to know since I was there. Since it was me who did most of the killing that day.

The beginning? For what you want to hear about, I reckon that's the day the McCandles gang rode into town.

Back then, Coalville was just a little one-dog town stuck way the h--- out in southern Idaho where God didn't get to very often. I'd been working for Sydney Hackett off and on for several years by then. Syd was the sheriff in Coalville, but he ran some cattle on the side, and it was my job every spring to run his cows up into the Black Pine Mountains northwest of us, then go fetch 'em home again in the fall.

It was right after the autumn gather in early November of 1879 that the McCandles gang showed up. I'd just come in myself, pushing about forty-five head of mostly Hereford stock, thirty-eight of them with white-faced calves trotting along at their mothers' sides. Herb Smith, who ran the livery, saw me coming, and walked out to open the gate to his largest corral. He helped me shoo the leaders inside, and the rest of the herd followed along without hesitation. Then he swung the gate shut and latched it. I can still hear his voice in my mind, like it was yesterday.

"We were beginning to wonder what'd happened to you, Joey," Herb said, folding his arms over the second-from-the-top rail of the corral to study the white- and rust-colored herd.

I reined up a few yards away but didn't get down. "They were scattered," I said. "I had to go all the way up the Hop Along to find 'em."

"It's a d---ed good thing you did, too," said a voice from behind me.

I grinned but didn't turn around. At the fence, Herb chuckled. "Syd, you've got a nose for cattle," he said.

"I've got a nose for money," the Coalville sheriff corrected. "Especially when it's mine." He slapped my knee as he passed, but didn't stop until he was leaning into the corral next to Herb. "They all there, Joey?" he asked, eyeing the herd the way a man might examine a prized bull he wanted to enter at the state fair.

You've probably noticed that both men referred to me as Joey, rather than Joe or Joseph. That's because I was still a kid then. That part of the legend is true. I was barely seventeen years old that summer, although I'd been on my own ever since my ma died when I was eight or so. Just about everyone in Coalville called me Joey, or did until I came back a couple of weeks later with Ian McCandles trussed to his saddle like a gutted deer, more dead than alive.

Syd was counting his cows and calves, and I could tell from the set of his shoulders that he was beginning to realize there was a sizable gap between the two.

"What happened?" he asked, turning to me with his brows furrowing up like a couple of woolly worms clinging to his forehead.

I recall squirming a bit at his question. Syd Hackett was the closest thing to family I had in Coalville, but he was blunt-spoken and short-tempered even on his good days. He was also uncommonly fond of the nest egg he was building with his side investment in cattle. To Syd, a lost calf wasn't just dead veal, it was a chunk of gold taken out of his pocket, and, from the way he sometimes acted, I've often wondered if one or two of those coins didn't occasionally root themselves under his skin. Like it wasn't just money a dead calf represented, but a piece of his own flesh.

"I found the cows, but not all of them were sucking," I said.

"I can see that, d---it. I asked what happened."

"A mountain lion is what happened," I shot back, irritated by the accusation in his tone. It wasn't me that raided his d---ed beeves.

"Painters butchered . . ."—Syd's gaze swept over the scattering cattle, his lips moving gently as he tallied the count—"*eight* calves?"

"Killed three that I know of. I found what was left of them in the rocks near the summit. I don't know what happened to the other five, but they weren't with their mamas."

You could almost see the air turning dark above Syd's head, like you'd expect at any moment to see a gust of stormy wind or tiny flashes of lightning along the brim of his hat. Quality yearlings like Syd's Herefords were fetching $12 a head in Salt Lake City that summer.

Squaring around, he said: "I hope you shot the son-of-a-b----."

"Yeah, I killed it."

My answer seemed to placate him a little. He cleared his throat as if to shake out some of the anger that had gathered there. "You got the skin?"

"Nope. Not after what happened two years ago."

A couple years back a similar situation had occurred. I finally managed to tree the guilty cat on a sheer granite bluff up near timberline, but when I shot it, it tumbled off the cliff's face into a rocky gorge a couple of hundred feet below. Leaving my horse tied to a sapling, I picked my way down through the rocks to recover the hide. It was when I came back up with the skin draped over my shoulder that all h--- broke loose. As soon as my horse caught a whiff of the painter's scent, it spooked and bolted, leaving behind a stripped and twisted sapling bent close to the ground, and me standing there with my jaw flopped down on my chest.

It didn't help to leave the dead cat's hide behind when I went after my mount, either. I guess the cougar's smell was all over me and my clothes by then. I couldn't get within fifty yards of that horse until I stripped down and bathed in the icy waters of the Hop Along. Had to wash my clothes down to my socks and long-handles, too. That's why I hadn't skinned the cat I'd shot this year. I didn't want to risk being left afoot again.

"Besides," I said. "Why should I bring in the hide? You're the one who'd collect the reward on it."

"My calves it was feeding on," Syd reminded me, but his words lacked their earlier heat. Following the direction of his gaze, I saw a cloud of dust on the road that led up from Kelton, down on the Central Pacific Railroad line in Utah. A shiver ran down my spine as I eyed that far-off plume of wispy soil. I didn't think much of it at the time, the weather having turned chilly several days before, but in looking back at it now, I've often wondered if what I experienced wasn't a premonition of some sort. I kind of think maybe it was.

You'd have to be familiar with Coalville and the lay of the land surrounding it to understand how we could see those horsemen from so far away. Coalville sat on the southeastern slope of the Black Pine Mountains, probably ten miles east of the main road that linked Kelton with the gold fields of western

15

Idaho. It had sprung up only a few years before when a vein of high-grade steam coal had been discovered protruding from a hillside twenty or so miles north of the Central Pacific line.

I don't recall any more who first busted out chunks of coal to sell to the railroad, or who sunk a shaft into the side of the hill to reach the larger deposits underneath. I do know it wasn't long before some conglomerate out of Salt Lake City bought the whole caboodle, right down to pick and bucket, and turned it into a thriving business. They named the mine the Hop Along, after the creek that flowed past less than one hundred yards away, and sent Big Ed Farmer up to manage the operation. If you know anything about coal mining in those days, that name will mean something to you.

Anyway, we were close enough to the Idaho/Utah border that, on a clear day, you could see the chimney smoke from Kelton, like a smeared thumbprint on the blue horizon. The Hop Along had an exclusive contract for its coal with the Central Pacific, and hauled nearly thirty tons of the stuff down to the Kelton depot every month.

Coalville itself sat near the top of a long, south-facing, mostly barren—if you didn't count rocks, sagebrush, or rattlesnakes— slope that stretched all the way to Kelton, and a good distance beyond. Because it was all downhill and mostly high desert, a single stagecoach or freight wagon could raise enough dust on a clear day to be seen from ten miles away. A group of horsemen, riding fast and close together like these were, could be seen from about half that distance.

I watched them for a moment, then looked at Syd. "What's got your hackles up?"

"Who said my hackles were up?"

But I could tell they were. Herb sensed it, too.

"There's been a stranger in town for a couple of days now, Joey," Herb said. "Nobody can figure him out."

"Maybe he's looking for work. Or maybe he's just passing through on his way to Boise City."

"He ain't looking for work," Syd kind of snarled. "And there's nothing in Coalville to keep him here."

"He rides a d---ed fine horse," Herb added, as if that meant something significant. "A tall sorrel with a flaxen mane and tail. She's a mare, which I wouldn't want for a trail horse, but she's got a deep chest and legs like pile drivers. I haven't seen her run, but I'll bet she's fast."

"She's too fine of a horse for a common drifter," Syd said.

"So you figure he's waiting for someone?" I asked. I was finally starting to understand why the two of them were acting so disquieted.

Syd moved away from the corral. "Put your horse up, Joey, then grab a bite to eat. Tell Jim to put it on my tab."

I didn't hesitate. My belly was already rumbling in anticipation of a hot meal, one not of my own inexperienced preparation.

I should probably mention here that the horse I was riding wasn't mine. Like the Herefords, it belonged to Syd. It was a dappled gray with an easy jog and an amiable personality, which isn't a bad trait for a horse to have when it's just the two of you off by yourselves for a couple of weeks. It wasn't much of a steed—I called it Hammerhead when Syd wasn't around—but it was everything I needed for no more cattle than I had to handle. Syd owned a second horse for personal use, a flashy palomino he'd brought with him from California when he came out here four or five years ago. I don't think Syd would have been caught dead on a ewe-necked runt like Hammerhead, but I liked the gray just fine.

I dismounted at the livery's wide front door and led the horse inside. After stripping the tack from his back, I turned him into a stall at the rear of the barn. I fed him and made sure he had plenty of water and fresh bedding, then curried him down while he ate. When I was finished caring for my horse—Syd's horse again, now that I was back in Coalville—I shouldered my saddle—that, at least, was mine—and carried it out behind the livery to the shack where I lived.

My home in those days was an old grain shed Herb used before building a tighter, roomier one inside his stables. It was just log walls with a wood floor and tin roof that slanted from front to back, maybe six feet deep by ten feet wide. I'd insulated the walls with discarded newspapers and chinked the bigger gaps with a mixture of mud and straw.

I had a small pot-bellied stove for heat in winter and an old military cot with a scraggly buffalo robe and several wool blankets for a bed. There was a three-legged table propped into the corner, an empty fruit crate for a chair, and a cowhide trunk with most of the hair rubbed off for storage. There was a window, too, although its glass was so dirty I could barely see out of it. Dead flies and mummified bees grown crunchy with age cluttered the sill, and spider webs decorated the exposed rafters.

Although it wouldn't be considered homey by many, back then it seemed like a palace to me. You've got to remember that I'd slept in empty hogsheads and under porches for a good portion of my early years, so I wasn't going to complain about a little dust or an occasional rodent.

After shouldering the door closed behind me, I dropped the saddle out of the way, then slid my rifle from its scabbard. It was an Evans lever-action, a .44 Long that I'd purchased a few years back, and I don't mind telling you it was my pride and joy. It had taken quite a beating at some point in its life. Syd said he thought the barrel had been shortened, as there was a homemade front sight tacked in just behind the muzzle, along with a deep scar in the wood of the forearm that couldn't be sanded out without deforming the silhouette. But those flaws were easily overlooked by the fourteen-year-old kid I was when I bought it, holding his first-ever firearm.

I leaned the rifle in the corner and dumped the contents of my saddlebags onto the cot. Picking out my cleaning gear, I went over the Evans like it was the Queen's silver. It was the first thorough scrubbing I'd given the piece since going out after Syd's cattle, and I was determined to see it spotless before I looked after my own needs.

The local café, like a lot of other businesses in Coalville, took part of its name from the mine that kept it in operation. Jim Sanders and his wife, Marta, owned the place. They called it the Hop On Inn. Jim insisted they planned to add an upper floor with lodging for paying customers someday to justify the "Inn" part of the title, but they hadn't yet gotten around to it.

Jim was standing at the café's front window when I came in. I could tell he'd been keeping an eye on the approaching horsemen the same way Herb Smith was, sitting in his cane-bottomed rocker in front of the livery fiddling with a pipe he never seemed to get around to lighting.

"Hey, Joey," Jim greeted half-heartedly.

"Hey yourself."

"Hungry?"

"I could likely eat a horse if you've got one fresh cooked."

Jim smiled faintly, but he didn't come back with any of his usual wisecracks, like: *We're fresh out of horse, but I've got some ass in back,* or *We're fresh out of horse, but we've got plenty of apples.*

Horse apples . . . get it?

"Have a seat," Jim said. "I'll get you some stew."

"Horse?" I asked, but he went on into the kitchen like he hadn't heard me.

The stew was beef, steaming warm from the stove. He served it with fresh-baked bread smeared with huckleberry jam and a crock mug of cold buttermilk. I dived in like I was half starved, and barely noticed Jim's return to the window to keep an eye on the Kelton road.

"Where's Syd?" he asked after a couple of minutes.

"I ain't seen him since I put up my horse. Syd's horse, I mean."

"I knew what you meant."

"Something wrong?"

"I don't know, Joey. I surely don't. Been a stranger parked in the Palace for a couple of days now. He's got everyone spooked."

The Coal Palace was Coalville's sole drinking establishment, named after the same fire-breathing stone that kept the rest of the town in business.

"What's he done that's so scary?" I asked.

"Nothing," Jim admitted. "Maybe that's the problem. That and the fact that you can almost see the meanness seeping out of him." He glanced my way. "Do me a favor, Joey. Stay out of the Palace tonight?"

Now, the Coal Palace did get rowdy at times, especially on Saturday nights after the miners had been paid off for their weekly labors and came into town wanting to blow off some steam. But this wasn't Saturday. I was pretty sure of that.

"Sure," I replied, knowing even as I said it that I wouldn't. Especially not with everyone acting so tender-footed about a bunch of strangers. You would have thought the James boys were coming to town, the way folks were behaving.

I went back to eating—another bowl of stew, two more mugs of buttermilk, and nearly a whole loaf of bread before my belly finally surrendered. Thanking Jim for the grub, I moseyed outside. It was getting late in the day. The sun, setting behind the Hop Along's slag heap, looked like a puppy's chewed-up orange ball, and the air was turning chilly. I pulled the collar of my jacket up around my ears and settled my cap more firmly on my head.

And that right there is something else you ought to understand about the real old West. We didn't all go around wearing ten-gallon hats and fancy spurs and leather gloves with fringed gauntlets. Fact is, I've never owned a pair of spurs in my life, and I've ridden quite a bit over parts of Idaho and Oregon.

What I did wear in those days were nearly all hand-me-downs—used clothing I'd either salvaged from back-yard clotheslines or, more and more of late, that I got from the back wall shelves of the Mercantile, where they kept their second-hand stuff. This was usually as payment for some chore Syd thought needed doing. I wore brogan shoes and an eight-piece wool cap with a creased leather brim, a canvas jacket over a faded blue wool shirt, and sturdy, copper-riveted trousers from the Levi Strauss Company out of San Francisco. I had work gloves minus the fringe and a heavy coat and extra socks back in the shack.

Jim followed me onto the boardwalk, but he acted like I wasn't there. I saw several other merchants standing outside their businesses, all of them facing south, and not one of them speaking or even acknowledging anyone else. I'll tell you, it gave me an eerie feeling to see them like that, like they could sense something evil approaching that I had no inkling of.

The horsemen, there were nine of them, were just coming into town, looking trail-worn but alert. I don't think you would have noticed anything unusual about them other than the light-colored linen dusters several of them wore, covering them from collar to boot strap. Their hats were wide-brimmed and low-crowned, as was the fashion of the day for those who could afford a genuine Boss of the Plains Stetson, variously colored and well broken-in—dented and sweat-stained like any workingman's hat would be. The men themselves were a scraggly lot, whiskered and weathered and cold-looking, but I knew that feeling myself, having just come down out of the Black Pines.

They reined in at the Palace like they'd trained for it, wheeling toward the hitching rails as a single unit, then stepping down from their saddles with a liquid grace. As they dismounted, a few of the dusters swung open to reveal small arsenals belted at their waists—revolvers and Bowie knives, cartridge belts filled with gleaming brass or copper. Rifles protruded from scabbards fastened to their saddles, and a couple of them had sawed-off shotguns tied behind their cantles, on top of their bedrolls.

Seeing all that armament made me appreciate the uneasiness that had been badgering the local townsfolk. It was pretty obvious these weren't your run-of-the-mill drifters, passing through on their way to somewhere else. These were men with a purpose, a grim one judging by the hardened expressions on their faces.

The strangers stomped their feet and swung their arms to loosen up. Probably half of them paused long enough to spit in the street, as if stating their opinion of the place. After taking a final, dismissive look around, they trooped inside. The door had barely been slammed shut before I took off for the saloon.

"Don't be a fool, Joey!" Jim called after me.

"I just want a peek," I said, being too young then to understand that there were some things best left unpeeked at.

The Coal Palace had batwing doors like a lot of saloons did in those days, but they had been pulled back on the inside when the autumn temperatures started to drop, latched out of the way of the big, solid double doors they used to lock the place up at night. The lower panes of the Palace's single front window were painted red to discourage scrutiny from the street by wives, mothers, and sweethearts. At least that was the excuse I've always heard for tinted bar windows. I couldn't say whether or not that was true, but I do know I would have needed a ladder to see inside that way.

I was nervous about going in blind, yet too curious to let the opportunity slip away. Opening the right-hand door, I stepped inside and shut it softly behind me.

The Palace was a long, narrow room of dark timber and cheap, flocked wallpaper. The bar ran the length of its right side, with felt-covered gaming tables and chairs scattered around the rest of the room. A faro table and chuck-a-luck cage were in back, both of them currently unoccupied. Carpeted stairs led to the second floor, where four of the town's five prostitutes worked. The fifth, if you're wondering, had her own place up close to the mine, a Paiute woman who had seen better days long before I got there, and charged accordingly.

The horsemen were crowded around a table close to the window, nearly surrounding a long-legged man in a new-looking white Stetson. They all had scowls as deep as old axe wounds creasing their faces.

Adam Hoffman owned the Palace, although I suspect he would have sold it fairly reasonably at the moment. He was approaching the front table with three bottles of rye whiskey in his left hand, a collection of shot glasses cradled like newborn kittens in his right arm. The whores were clustered at the far end of the bar, Lucy among them.

If you've heard some version of this story before, you already know about Lucy Lytle. You're probably also thinking she was a dazzling, golden-haired angel who had accepted her lot in life only to support a destitute mother, a blind father, and anywhere from six to sixteen orphaned siblings, most of them maimed in one fashion or another. I've also heard she was a schoolmarm, a clerk in the local dry-goods store, a bank teller, and a dressmaker—figments like as not constructed out of some author's desire to avoid the obvious taint of admitting she was a hooker.

Truth is, she did have a brother down in Salt Lake City with an arm so badly mangled in a fall from the second-story balcony of a whorehouse that it never did heal properly. The fact that he'd been too drunk at the time to seek medical attention no doubt contributed to his disability. Lucy didn't support him, and never had that I'm aware of, financially or otherwise. In fact, she'd once confided to me that the world would have been a better place if he'd broken his neck in that tumble, instead of just his arm.

Lucy claimed she was a dewy-eyed seventeen-year-old when she came to Coalville, the same age as I was. I believed her because . . . well, I guess I believed her because I was seventeen myself, and prone to swallowing lies from pretty women. Looking back, I'd hazard she was closer to thirty than twenty. She was skinny and small-breasted, not unattractive by any means, but not the ravishing beauty some of the periodicals have made her out to be. She had dark curly hair that would kink up in damp weather, green eyes, and a crooked front tooth that was always darker than those around it. She was as pale as whey and coarse-spoken, but I liked her. I liked her a lot, and I guess you can figure out why without me spelling it out for you.

There were three or four others in the saloon when I slipped inside. A teamster we all called Drunk Charlie was slumped at a table near the rear of the room, next to some of the night-shift crew from the Hop Along, their faces nearly black from their labors in the mines. Everyone except Drunk Charlie looked as jumpy as a fat-legged frog in a French restaurant.

As soon as I walked in, Lucy motioned me over to where she and the other whores were standing. I passed within ten feet of Adam Hoffman, but he didn't even glance at me. Those boys at the table sure did, though. Their eyes pried at every wrinkle and gap in my clothing, looking for some kind of hide-out weapon. If any of them noticed the outline of the stubby clasp knife in my jeans pocket, they didn't seem intimidated by it.

Lucy grabbed me and spun me around, standing behind me with her hands on my shoulders. I might have wished she was doing that for the security I offered, but I knew she was just keeping me in reach so that I didn't get underfoot. She seemed aggravated by my presence.

"What's going on?" I asked her.

"Hush! You shouldn't even be here."

"I wanted to see what was going on."

Her nails dug into my shoulders deep enough to hurt, and she gave me a quick shake. "Shut up, d--- it," she said, although I'd like to think it wasn't without a certain amount of affection.

After dropping off his cargo of bottle and glass, Adam Hoffman beat a hasty retreat to the sober side of the bar. At the table, a couple of cold-looking gents in grimy dusters were seating themselves in front of the man in the white hat. I could tell right away that White Hat was the stranger everyone had been so agitated over. His nose wasn't red or drippy like those of the other men, and his cheeks lacked the freshly burnished sheen of a Western wind.

They started talking low, but I could sense the heat in their voices from across the room. Finally one of the men slammed his clenched fist down on top of the table and said: "Because that's where you said you'd be, god d---it!"

White Stetson shrugged. "I didn't feel comfortable there."

"You make a plan, Ian, you stick to it," the first man said.

"I disagree," the man in the white Stetson—Ian—replied. "You've got to remain flexible in this line of work if you don't want to risk getting your neck stretched."

Someone growled unintelligibly, and another man said: "There'd better be a d---ed good reason you came here, instead of meeting us at Cedar Junction."

"Why, Happy Collins, that sounds disturbingly like a threat," Ian replied mildly.

Lucy gasped softly in my ear, and there was a quick murmur of alarm from the Hop Along miners. My own pulse broke into

25

a lope. Happy Collins isn't as well-known today as men like Cole Younger or Billy the Kid, but he was famous enough in that time and place to bring a chill to just about anyone's heart. Especially when you realized you were in the same room with him. Collins was widely known as a shootist and thief, and I had it on fairly good authority that he'd earned his moniker during a California stagecoach robbery when he'd laughed hysterically while gunning down a trio of stubborn passengers who didn't want to give up their wallets.

"A threat is exactly what it is, McCandles," Happy said.

Let me tell you, *that* got everyone's attention. Ian McCandles didn't have the same man-killer reputation as Happy Collins, but he was still a highly feared individual, and rightly so. McCandles was a known stage and bank robber who operated across Idaho, Utah, Nevada, and Oregon, and he was considered a very dangerous man to cross. Unless you were someone like Happy Collins, I guess.

Lordy, Ian McCandles and Happy Collins in Coalville's own Palace Saloon. That meant the others would be just as wicked, and I searched their faces wonderingly. From what I knew of Idaho's outlaw element, I was pretty certain the dark-skinned half-breed in moccasins would have to be Yakima Tom Candy, a well-known bandit in that area throughout much of the 1870s. But what about Jud Linderman or Carl Baily or Ben Ryder? Did they stand among these wind-blown riders? I'll tell you, it made my scalp crawl just thinking about it.

Glancing deliberately in our direction, McCandles said: "Let's discuss this matter privately, gentlemen, after we've all had a drink. Reuben, shove that bottle over here."

Reuben Stanton! It had to be!

I felt Lucy's fingers drilling into my shoulders like tiny, steel-tipped augers. One of the whores—I didn't see which—whimpered softly; another one told her to suck it in. I guess she didn't want any attention drawn their way, but she might as well have wished she could walk through a rainstorm and not get wet. Five pale-skinned, scantily dressed women in shiny satin huddled at the far end of the bar like a clutch of baby chicks was hardly camouflage.

Chairs scraped loudly across the floor as the rest of the outlaw gang—mind you, I was only assuming then that banditry was everyone's occupation, although that speculation was soon put to rest—pulled up seats, then plopped into them the way men did when they'd been too long in the saddle. I started to slide away, but Lucy hauled me back. "You just stay put," she whispered none too gently in my ear.

"I've got to tell Syd what's going on."

"Syd'll find out what's going on soon enough, if he hasn't already. You stand still and keep your mouth shut."

Lucy's motherly assumption of jurisdiction irritated me, even though I knew she was only doing it out of concern for my safety. But it made me mad, and it still does when someone tells me not to speak up or get involved, to stand like sheep waiting for slaughter while evil is perpetrated around us.

I reckon that's why I eventually ended up in City of Rocks, along with Lucy Lytle, Della Wilson, and what was left by then of the McCandles gang.

Those Notorious Badmen of Southwestern Idaho
BY MALCOMB COMBS
SIX FALLS PRESS, 1921

[One] of Idaho's most feared bandits of the late 19th Century was Ian Bartholomew McCandles, a transplanted Californian who migrated to the Boise City mining camps in the early 1870s. . . . [McCandles was] known to have committed six murders along the western slopes of the Sierra-Nevada Mountains in his early years . . . later became leader of a loosely organized gang of thugs and murderers operating out of the Owyhee and Humbolt river regions of southwestern Idaho and portions of Nevada and Oregon.

William Jared "Happy" Collins was renowned for what many have insisted was his nervous laughter emitted during the commission of particularly violent crimes. Collins . . . was a native of Georgia, reportedly an under-age citizen of Atlanta during Sherman's triumphant march on that city . . . said to have murdered indiscriminately during acts of robbery . . . an occasional member of the McCandles Gang (see page 47, Badmen).

Probably the most cold-blooded killer the region had to endure during that era was Judah Linderman . . . little is known of Linderman's past before his arrival in Southwestern Idaho in 1875 or 1876 . . . [he is] reported to have killed a man in Twin Falls because he "didn't care for the sound of the man's laughter" after an off-color joke was made in a downtown saloon.

. . . [H]orse thief Ben Ryder was also a known accomplice of the Ian McCandles gang . . . [some] reports claim he was killed in South America with the Sundance Kid and Butch Cassidy, although most accounts agree Ryder would have been well into his sixties by that date . . . historians argue that it is unlikely Ryder was in Bolivia at that time.

Carl Baily was said to have the innocent mien of a newborn, yet it is claimed he killed thirteen men in his career as a bank and stagecoach robber . . . fled to Boise City from New Mexico after murdering a popular sheriff there in 1872. . . .

Yakima Tom Candy . . . gunrunner and whiskey trader to the desert tribes of eastern Nevada and southern Oregon . . . said to have killed more men than any other in Idaho's notoriously bloody history save for the baby-faced murderer Carl Baily . . . nothing more is known . . . of Yakima Tom.

SESSION TWO

I don't guess there's much point in relating everything that happened in the Coal Palace over the next few hours. There was a lot of anger toward McCandles about someone named Long Pete, who was no longer with them, a lot of fast drinking, glass slamming, and glowering looks. The tension in that room was like a physical weight bearing down upon everyone.

Lucy and the other whores in particular were becoming more anxious as the evening deepened into dusk and Adam made his way around the room lighting lamps. The more the McCandles bunch drank, the more their attention kept shifting toward the women. Several of the men were grinning with hard-edged anticipation. Ian was keeping a rein on them, but just barely. They didn't seem to pay any attention to the others until one of the miners stood up to make his way to the front door.

"Where you goin', a--hole?" Reuben Stanton barked.

The miner flinched as if he'd been stung by a bee. "I gotta get ready for my shift," he said.

"Sit down," Reuben ordered. "You're taking the night off."

The miner glanced uncertainly at his buddies, until Happy said: "You was told to sit down, tin pan. You'd best do it."

"Yessir," the miner said, running the two words together as he practically jumped backward into his chair.

Reuben eyed the table of pick-and-shovel men like he had something especially devilish percolating in his brain, and the miners were all well aware of it. Sweat streaked the coal dust on their faces, and their eyes seemed to be fastened solidly to the table top directly in front of them. I thought something was surely going to pop until Ian said loudly: "Boys, we need some grub."

The outlaws turned to look at him. Reuben, too, although more slowly than the rest. Ian stabbed a finger in my direction. "You!"

Something in my stomach went plop, and I swayed back feeling suddenly light-headed. I'd just been thinking how if I'd been that miner, I wouldn't have taken the kind of guff Reuben Stanton had dished on him, yet the very first words out of my mouth were: "Yessir?"

It must have been the high-pitched break at the end of my reply that caused McCandles's men to laugh out loud. A man in a dirty frock coat and smudged linen shirt said: "Mister McCandles seeks your recommendations regarding local dining establishments, lad. Have you a suggestion?"

"No, I ain't asking him about no d---ed dining establishment," Ian shot back. "I'm asking him who serves a decent meal in this s--- hole of a town."

"Don't confuse the kid with fancy talk, Jack," Happy chided.

Jack? Fancy talk and once-elegant clothes, a ruby ring on his finger that gleamed like a thimble of fresh blood in the flickering lamplight, a smile wide enough to make even the most hardened whore swoon like a Southern belle? That could only be Gentleman Jack Conner, and my, oh my, didn't my brain reel from that bit of revelation? Gentleman Jack had a reputation for courtesy that some claimed belied a simpleton's mind and a killer's instinct; others insisted he treated everyone with respect because he refused to accept anything less himself. Once I got to know him better, I leaned toward the latter explanation, but with a murderer's soul.

They were all staring at me, waiting, I finally realized, for a

31

reply. "There's the Hop On Inn, just up the street," I managed to croak out.

"And do you recommend the cuisine there?" Jack inquired.

"I ain't never had any cuisine, but the stew's good."

A couple of the outlaws laughed again at my response, although it would be a few more years before I understood what they found so humorous.

Smiling affably Gentleman Jack said: "Would you be so kind as to ask the proprietor of the Hop On Inn if he might administer us our sustenance here tonight?"

While I was struggling to translate that into everyday Coalville, Ian said: "What friend Conner here is tryin' to say is for you to go fetch us some grub, and be quick about it."

Lucy whispered in my ear: "Don't come back, Joey. Stay with Jim and Marta."

"I'll be back as soon as I can," I told Ian, and Lucy gave me a stinging cuff to my ear, like a mama bear chastising its cub.

"Boy, I believe that gal has got a spark for you," Happy observed with a leer.

If she did, she had a peculiar way of showing it, I thought as I rubbed my tender lobe.

It had come onto full dark while I was in the Palace, but I noticed there weren't many lamps showing around town. Folks were keeping low, I supposed. I hurried up the street to the café, but paused outside when I noticed its darkened interior. Warily I shoved the door open.

"Joey!" Jim grabbed my arm and yanked me inside, and the door was slammed shut behind me.

From the boardwalk I had thought the place to be without light, but I saw now that there must have been a lamp or lantern in the back room, its wick turned low. In its faint illumination I recognized several other men and a few women scattered around the room. None of them was sitting or eating.

"Who are they?" Herb demanded tersely.

"It's the McCandles gang," I said, and Marta gasped and cupped her fingers over her mouth. She wasn't the only one taken aback by the news. Despite the presence of ladies, several of the townsmen uttered curses that dripped apprehension like soup from a mustache.

"I figured it was something like that," said Big Ed Farmer. "What do they want, Joey?"

"Right now they want food, and they want me to bring it to them. They've got some of your men in there, too, Mister Farmer. They tried to leave, but Reuben and Happy wouldn't let them."

My announcement brought a murmur of alarm to the room. Once I'd identified Ian McCandles, the rest just fell naturally into place in that part of the country. Reuben Stanton, Happy Collins. They'd likely figure out Gentleman Jack Conner and Yakima Tom were in there, too, given a few minutes to ponder it.

Big Ed rubbed his bearded chin thoughtfully. "That'd be Mick, Cam, and Jeff. I sent the night crew into the mine, but I've kept the day shift confined to their barracks."

Big Ed was a former military officer, but it was the Hop Along's owners in Salt Lake City who had decided to furnish living quarters and a mess hall for the miners—at a charge taken from their weekly pay, of course. It was a sound business decision for the mine's owners, not so much so for the town's businessmen.

"What should we do?" Burt Newman asked. Burt was the town's barber, although he also filled in as both doctor and mortician when the need arose. Small towns had to make do as best they could in those days.

"I'd say we'd better give them what they want, before they come and take it," Jim said.

33

"I agree," Herb added. "Unless we want to go up against a bunch of killers, I don't see where we have much choice."

"Where's Syd?" I asked.

"He ain't here," Big Ed replied, acting put out.

"He's around somewhere," Herb said in the sheriff's defense.

"Yeah, where? Hiding under his bunk?"

"Syd'll be here," I replied, getting my dander up at Big Ed's implication. "He's probably trying to decide the best way to handle this without anyone getting hurt."

"Lay off of Syd Hackett," Jim told Big Ed, mostly for my benefit, I suspect. He turned to his wife. "Get a bucket, hon, and we'll put some stew in it, then send along some spoons and bowls. I'll get what bread we've got left, maybe some butter and jam."

"They were asking about coosy," I said.

"Coosy?"

"Something like that."

"Well, we don't serve it here," Jim replied. "I've never heard of it. They'll have to settle for stew or go somewhere else."

While Jim and Marta were putting together a supper for the gunmen, the others began interrogating me about what was going on in the saloon. They were afraid the outlaws were there to rob the town, and never mind the fact that Coalville didn't really have anything worth stealing. There were no banks or wealthy citizens or valuable ores like gold or silver. This was a coal mining town, its riches fit for nothing more exciting than a stove or a Central Pacific locomotive. I answered their questions as best I could for several minutes, until the Hop Along's head clerk, Harvey Brandt, slipped inside to announce that a couple of members of the McCandles gang were rummaging around in Herb Smith's livery.

Naturally everyone surged to the window. I went along, caught up in the tide. Standing next to me, his mouth opening and closing several times, Herb finally blurted: "Wh—, what are they doing in my livery?"

"I'd guess they're looking for fresh horses," Big Ed said.

Herb swore under his breath. We all knew right away that Big Ed was right. We'd seen the horses the McCandles gang had ridden in on. Good mounts all, but worn down and gaunted up, like they'd been pushed hard.

"They won't want nags or mules, either," Burt said. "You got anything over there they'd be interested in?"

"H---, yes, I've got some fine stock in there. I've got Ed's bay and those sorrels I picked up in Kelton last spring, a d---ed fine chestnut gelding. . . ." His words trailed off as he did a mental inventory of the livestock in his care.

"Where the h--- is Syd?" Harvey asked. "Shouldn't he be here doing . . . something?"

A quick muttering shoved through the crowd like a rude customer, quite a bit lower and angrier than earlier, when all McCandles's men had seemed to want was food. If the outlaws were starting to fan out across town, nothing would be safe.

"If Syd wants to keep that badge he's wearing, he'd d---ed well better show up soon," Big Ed stated flatly.

Although I wanted to say something in support of Syd, I didn't figure it would do much good. People were starting to panic, and when that happens, you can generally kiss logic good bye. Besides, I was beginning to wonder myself where Syd had gotten to. It wasn't like him to be tardy when trouble was present.

My eyes had adjusted to the murky quality of the room, so it was startling when the light dimmed even more. We all turned as Burt returned from the kitchen carrying a glass lamp, its wick turned so low it was guttering toward extinction. "No point in attracting attention to ourselves," he said almost apologetically.

"Smartest thing I've heard so far," someone I couldn't identify replied, and Burt leaned over the lamp's tall chimney to blow the flame out altogether, plunging the room into darkness.

"Smarter yet," the unknown gent added.

With the lamp extinguished, we had a better view of the street. I watched as a couple of McCandles's men came out of the livery leading several horses between them. They took them over to the Palace, where they began switching saddles. Syd's palomino was among them, causing my fists to clench in helplessness. Where was Syd?

A clatter of tin and pottery intruded upon our quiet observations, and we pivoted as one at Jim and Marta's return. Jim motioned me over.

"This is all the stew we've got, Joey," he said, handing me a hefty wicker basket. "All the bread, too."

"I'll tell them," I replied.

Then Herb said, as if the thought had just occurred to him: "Wait a minute. We can't send Joey back there. He's just a kid."

Dead silence greeted Herb's words, followed by an uneasy cough from somewhere deeper in the room. It might have been as dark as pitch in there, but I recognized most of their voices, including Big Ed Farmer's.

"I reckon he's old enough, Herb."

"No, he isn't," Jim said, glancing at Marta as if seeking her confirmation. I noticed she ignored him.

"I can do it," I told them. "They're expecting me, anyway."

"Let him go," Harvey said. "If they're expecting him and someone else shows up, they might get mad. Might even shoot whoever we did send over."

Jim reached half-heartedly for the wicker basket, but I swung it away from his outstretched paw. While the others argued silently with their consciences, I opened the door and stepped outside. I might have expected someone to say something, even if it was just—"Good luck, kid."—but nobody uttered a word as I pulled the door closed behind me.

I paused on the boardwalk long enough to tug my cap down, then headed for the saloon. The outlaws had finished switching tack from their worn-out mounts to the fresh horses. I thought they'd all gone inside, but, as I drew near the saloon's front doors, a shadow detached itself from the wall. For a moment, hope soared in my breast as I imagined Syd stepping forward to prevent me from entering the Palace. Then I realized the shadow was too short and blocky to be the sheriff, and the stranger's voice, when he spoke, was unfamiliar.

"Who're you?"

"Joey Roper. I've got the food. . . ."

"Shut up and get in there." He jerked the door open and a shaft of lamplight darted outside to illuminate a pair of grease-blackened moccasins.

I stepped through the door, and Yakima Tom closed it on my heels. It didn't take long to realize something had changed while I was away, and not for the better. The tension inside the Palace made what I'd felt earlier seem like skimmed milk. I counted the whores and came up two short. Fortunately Lucy was still there, sitting at a table with Adam Hoffman and another hooker named Ruby Davidson. A couple of hardcases were also missing, and my gaze was pulled to the carpeted steps leading upstairs.

The door opened behind me and Yakima Tom slipped inside, quiet as a shadow.

"Nobody followed him. Ain't nobody movin' around out there no more."

"I didn't figure they would," Ian said, sloped back in his chair like he owned the place. "They're too scared. Ain't that right, kid?"

"They're skittish, for a fact," I said.

"They'd better stay that way, too," Happy growled, like the fault would be mine if they didn't. He yanked the basket out of my hand and set it on a table. "What'd they send us?"

"Some stew and bread and butter."

"By God, if it's warm, that sounds good," one of the gunmen said. "It'd better be warm, though," he added, glaring at me as if that, too, would be my fault if it wasn't.

"Ol' Rand's belly's been thinkin' it was forgot," another outlaw commented.

Randall Anderson. I'd heard of him, as well.

Happy gave me a shove toward the door. "Git on home, boy. We've got grown-up business to attend to here, and we don't need you underfoot while we're at it."

I looked at Lucy, and I guess my eyes must have betrayed my feelings, because Happy started laughing.

"Don't worry, sonny, we ain't gonna do nothing to her that ain't been done a hundred times before," he said.

"Get out of here, Joey," Lucy said tautly.

"No, keep him around for a while," Reuben Stanton said. "We might need him again."

"I told him to go," Happy said, his smile dropping from his face. Putting a hand on my chest, he gave me another shove, hard enough this time that I nearly fell. *"Git!"*

I backed reluctantly toward the door, my gaze touching briefly upon Lucy, Adam, Ruby, and the three Hop Along miners sitting quietly at the rear of the room. They reminded me of a drummer I'd once seen at the Hop On Inn, the stricken look on his face just seconds before the food he was eating came back up. Only Drunk Charlie looked unperturbed, but I doubt if he even knew what was going on.

I paused with my hand on the knob to see if Reuben would insist that I stay, but he was rooting obliviously through the wicker basket alongside Rand. I took a last look at Lucy, who motioned with her eyes for me to go, then I opened the door and stepped outside.

I'll tell you what, right at that moment I felt about as low and cowardly as a seventeen-year-old can get. Part of me wanted to go back inside and make things right, but I knew that was just a kid's bravado. There was only one person in Coalville that night who had not only the courage to face down the McCandles gang, but the skill. I just didn't have the vaguest idea where he was at the moment.

I studied the horses hitched at the rails, all of them fresh and ready to ride the minute the outlaws finished their entertainment. The mounts the bandits had ridden in on had been set free, and most of them had wandered across the street to graze on the tall grass below Herb Smith's big corral, where Syd's cattle were bedded for the night. I don't know why I took all that in. Maybe it was my thoughts struggling for direction. If so, Syd's cattle weren't offering any new insights. I finally turned up the street toward the Hop On Inn, my shoulders sloped like a barn's roof.

The café was still dark when I got back, but the crowd inside had swollen to nearly twice its earlier size. The air had grown thicker, too, and there was a new odor that I now realize was fear, permeating the room. Big Ed grabbed me as soon as I walked in and yanked me to the side.

"What's going on down there, Joey? What do they want?"

Others chimed in, the heart of their questions being much the same as before. I think Big Ed's clerk, Harvey Brandt, summed it up best.

"Did they come here to rob the mine payroll?"

"I didn't know the payroll at the Hop Along was worth robbing," I said, feeling scratchy all of a sudden.

A moment of stunned silence greeted my reply. Then Big Ed's grip tightened on my shoulder. "Don't get smart, Roper, or I'll box your d---ed ears for you."

"If you want to box somebody's ears, go down to the Palace and take a swing at Ian McCandles," I said.

"Joey," Marta Sanders gasped. "What's gotten into you?"

"Leave him be, Ed," Jim said sharply. "Joey's gone into the Palace twice tonight. I'd say that's earned him the right to tell his story the way he sees fit."

"Brazen little wood's colt," Big Ed grumbled, then gave me a shove reminiscent of the one Happy Collins had given me in the Palace.

"Good Lord, boys!" someone at the front door exclaimed. "It's Hackett."

At his words, the whole crowd slid toward the front window like a single-celled entity. I was among them, squeezed in and pressed so tightly against the glass that my breath fogged the pane. Sure enough, there was Syd, striding purposefully across the street toward the Palace. The moon wasn't quite up yet, but there were stars aplenty shining in the sky, and I could see that Syd was well-heeled. He carried his big Peacemaker holstered on his right side, and had a second revolver tucked inside his belt. A sawed-off double-barreled 10-gauge was cradled across the elbow of his left arm, while his right hand gripped the deadly weapon just behind its twin hammers. I knew Syd could snick those mule-ears back with one easy swipe of his thumb, and blast a hole through the middle of h--- a second later. Yet I found little comfort in that knowledge.

Now, you might imagine from the way I've spoken of Syd Hackett so far that I would have swelled up with pride to see him out there like that, but what I felt instead was something akin to a chunk of ice dropped down my gullet. I wondered if Syd knew what he was getting into, the character of the men gathered at the Palace. Surely he didn't intend to face them down alone. Yet who else could he turn to? Big Ed Farmer?

Herb Smith? Huh! Not too d---ed likely, I thought.

A feeling of panic welled up inside of me, and I began pushing for the door. "Get out of my way!" I cried, shoving at the
weight of humanity that seemed bent on holding me back as
firmly as chains. "Move!"

"Stay here, Joey," Herb said, grabbing me from behind.

"I've got to help him," I said, squirming wildly.

"Syd knows what he's doing. If he thought he needed help,
he would've asked for it."

I don't know if Herb really believed that or not, but I knew
in my heart that it was a lie. More than likely Syd had been
waiting up at the jail north of the livery all along for someone to
come over and offer him a hand. But no one had gone. Just as
no one had stopped me from delivering a basket of bread and
stew to the saloon. Everyone was afraid. *Everyone.* Even Big Ed
Farmer, who some said was the toughest son-of-a-b---- in
Coalville, and had men from his own crew inside.

"Let me go, d---it," I wailed, struggling even harder, but the
townsmen had suddenly turned into responsible adults regarding my safety.

"It's too dangerous, Joey," Burt Newman said.

"Those are some hard men over there, kid," Harvey Brandt
added. "You'd best stay here where we can keep an eye on
you."

Right at that moment, I think I despised just about every living soul in Coalville. Sure as h--- I despised the hypocrites who
had me surrounded inside the Hop On Inn. I felt like bawling
from helplessness. Then someone opened the front door and
several of the men moved onto the boardwalk for a better look.
That was all the opportunity I needed. I brought the heel of my
shoe down on Herb's instep just as hard as I could. Howling
like a lovelorn wolf, the liveryman fell back into the arms of
those behind him. As soon as his fingers slid from my shoulders,

I ducked low and made a break for the door. By the time anyone knew what was going on, I was halfway down the block.

Syd had already disappeared into the Palace. I slowed my reckless approach when the closed front doors appeared before me. For a minute, I didn't know what to do. Should I just walk on in? Or should I slip around back and try to sneak in through the rear door or a window? While I stood there waffling back and forth, a loud crash from within abruptly terminated my indecision. Giving up any notion of stealth, I rushed to the front entrance. Although I hesitated a moment with my hand on the iron knob to see if I could hear anything from inside, a deep silence seemed to have fallen over the Palace. I pushed open the door and stepped inside.

"God d---!" Happy Collins yelled, whirling toward me like a striking rattlesnake. I jerked to a stop, my eyes glued to the yawning bore of the bandit's revolver leveled at the bridge of my nose.

"Hold off," Ian snapped. "It's just the kid."

"I told you to get the h--- outta here, boy," Happy snarled.

As calmly as I could, I shut the door behind me. Movement stirred at my side, but there was no noise. Not even the scuff of leather on wood. An iron-like fist circled my left bicep, and I found myself gawking into the face of Yakima Tom Candy. I'll tell you what, that guy could just flat float when he wanted to.

Yakima Tom hauled me over to the table where McCandles and Gentleman Jack Conner were seated. The rest of the McCandles gang was scattered around the room. Syd stood near the end of the bar, his shotgun still riding the bend of his elbow. The look Syd gave me as I stumbled past in Yakima Tom's grip could have boiled water.

McCandles turned back to Syd. "You never did say what brought you here, lawman."

"I came for my horse," Syd said. "Guess I might as well pick up the others while I'm at it. Unless you boys want to pay for them."

McCandles leaned back in his chair and chuckled. "Now, I call that a plucky attitude for a man in your predicament, and d---ed admirable for a lawman. But I don't have your horse, friend."

I took a quick glance at the table where Adam Hoffman sat and was relieved to see that Lucy was still at his side. All of the whores were there, although a couple of them looked quite a bit worse for wear than the last time I'd seen them. Big Ed's miners sat at the next table over, as cowed as kittens, and I figured, if it came to a fight, they'd be just about as useless, too.

Still acting as nonchalant as a man sitting down to a well-earned meal, Syd remarked: "I believe you do, friend. It's that palomino hitched out front. Fact of the matter is, all of those horses out there belong to someone here in Coalville."

"I reckon not," Reuben Stanton said coldly.

A muscle twitched faintly in Syd's cheek, and I knew he was growing impatient. That little tic was a thing I'd learned to watch for over the years, and to make myself scarce whenever I saw it. I don't know if McCandles or any of his men picked up on it or not, but I doubt if it would have changed their minds about the horses.

"I won't let strangers ride into my town and steal livestock without consequence," Syd said.

"That's a provocative accusation, friend, though likely based on ignorance," Ian replied calmly. "The fact is, we ain't stealing those horses. We're just trading our wore-out mounts for fresh ones. Give them ponies we leave behind a few days to rest up, and your good citizens will consider themselves fairly dealt."

"I reckon not," Syd replied in the same tone of voice Reuben had used earlier.

"I beg a question," Gentleman Jack interrupted. "Are you

aware of our identities, sir?"

"I am," Syd said. "You're that bunch of chicken thieves that calls itself the McCandles gang. Half of you are wanted in three territories, including this one, for murder, rape, and robbery. But I'll give you boys a break. Ride out of here on your own horses, and I won't open up on you with this ten-gauge."

Nobody spoke for nearly a minute. Watching McCandles, I saw wariness creep into his demeanor, maybe even a glimmer of respect. "You've got b---s, lawman, I'll say that for you. I take it you've had good luck in the past facing men down with that scatter-gun?"

"There aren't many who'll spit in the eye of a man toting a double-barreled shotgun," Syd replied matter-of-factly. "I figure you boys have been in the game long enough to know what a couple of handfuls of double-ought buck would do at this range."

Several of McCandles's men exchanged nervous glances. Not Ian, though. Yakima Tom didn't seem especially worried, either. I guess holding me in front of him like a scrawny shield made him feel safe.

Frankly I was wishing right then that I'd listened to Herb and Jim when they told me to stay away from the Palace. I'd put Syd in a perilous situation by coming in here and allowing myself to be captured. He didn't act like he was going to let my being there sway his position, though.

"What about it, boys?" Syd said. "Is it worth risking your lives for?"

I don't know what kind of response I was expecting, but it sure as h--- wasn't Happy Collins kicking a chair out of his way and going for his revolver. Even parked in the shadows at the end of the bar like he was, I could see Syd's face go chalk white. His bluff had been called, maybe for the first time.

I made a vain attempt to twist free of Yakima Tom's grip, but he jerked me back. Just like I figured he would. Just like Big Ed Farmer had done in the Hop On Inn. Only this time, I was prepared. I let momentum spin me back and around, and, as it did, I kicked out as hard as I could for Yakima's shin. I caught it square, too. Yakima hollered loudly just as Happy's revolver and Syd's shotgun let off a combined roar that nearly knocked me off my feet.

Some years back a traveling salesman tried to bet me $5 that he could snuff the flames of two candles from across the room with a single shot from a revolver—while *blindfolded,* mind you. I didn't fall for it, though, recalling what happened that night in the Palace when the percussion from all those firearms going off almost as one snuffed out every last flame in the saloon.

The room went dark. Gunfire thundered like dynamite in my ears, so deafening I could barely hear all the screaming and shouting. Muzzles flashed, catching the erupting madness in brief, frozen acts, like the early flicker shows that used to travel the country. The smell of spent gunpowder was suffocating.

I grabbed Yakima Tom and tried to wrestle him to the floor, but I might as well have tried to hang onto a bucket of oil thrown into the air. He slipped free just that easily, and I stumbled and fell to my knees. Reaching out like a blind sinner pleading for salvation, I searched the darkness for the half-breed's arm. My reward was something hard and heavy slammed into my skull. My world exploded in a brilliant flash of pure white that quickly shrunk as if being sucked down a giant hole, dragging me with it.

Session Three

I saw a Tex Ritter movie down at the Rialto a couple of months ago where the hero got hit on the head and knocked out colder than an outhouse seat in January. Then, after the bad guy made his escape, the actor regained consciousness, jumped to his feet, and dashed outside. He saw the bad guy riding out of town at a gallop, so he jumped on his own horse and took off after him.

Hogwash!

Let me tell you what happens after you regain consciousness from a blow to the back of your skull with the barrel of a Colt revolver. The first thing you do is try to remember who the h--- you are. Then you start to wonder about all those faces spinning above you like planets flung free of their orbits. Then you puke. A lot. After you're done emptying your guts into the street—that's where I was when I came to, on the street in front of the Coal Palace—you just lay back and wish you could die. For me, I didn't really begin to regain my senses until I woke up a second time in the back room of Burt Newman's barbershop.

You might recall earlier that I said Burt also filled in as Coalville's medical consultant and mortician when the need arose? Well, he was playing doctor that night, and with about as much knowledge of the subject as I had. No, that's not true. Or at least it's not fair to Burt. I guess I'm still pretty bitter about everything that happened that night. The fact is, Burt did his best by everyone, and since Coalville didn't have a doctor at the

It wasn't quite as horrible as I'd expected from Burt's terse description, but it was bad enough. The Coal Palace had been gutted by fire, its windows all busted out, the wood surrounding the empty sockets scorched black as mascara. Gray smoke curled from the rubble, and the stink of wet ash hung over the town like a fog.

The buildings on either side of the Palace had been blackened by flames, but were otherwise undamaged. The same couldn't be said for the rest of the town. Bullet holes pocked just about every storefront along the street, and there weren't many windows that didn't sport a couple of bullet-shattered panes. The trampled body of a dog lay in the middle of the street, and in the big corral behind Herb's livery, several of Syd's Herefords had been shot and were already starting to bloat.

I was still standing numbly in the middle of the street when I heard someone come up behind me. "How are you feeling, Joey?" asked Herb Smith.

I didn't even turn around. "What happened?"

"Things got crazy after they shot Syd. They threw you and him outside, but wouldn't let anyone get near you. There was a lot of hollering and shouting, and every once in a while one or two of them would come outside to shoot up the town. I think they wanted to keep us pinned down. They ransacked the Mercantile for food and ammunition, then rode out about midnight after setting fire to the Palace."

"They shot Syd," I said numbly. I don't know why I said it. We both already knew how serious his wounds were. I guess I was still feeling a little dazed, although I couldn't have said whether it was from the blow I'd taken to the back of my head or from the shock of seeing Coalville pillaged.

"They shot several people," Herb said. "Two of Big Ed's night crew were killed. So was Ruby Davidson. Drunk Charlie was shot in the hand, although he wouldn't let Burt look at it.

He's already pulled out with his wagons for Kelton. Said he'd send a doctor when he got there. He probably will if he doesn't pass a saloon first."

"What about Lucy?"

"They, well, I'm afraid they took Lucy with them, Joey."

My guts had been feeling twitchy ever since waking up. Now they threatened to erupt like one of those volcanoes you read about in the newspapers. I walked over to the boardwalk and sat down, my head spinning so badly I had to squeeze my eyes shut to keep from falling over.

Herb sank down beside me. "I know you liked her, Joey, but she'll be all right."

That brought my eyes wide open. I looked at Herb like Burt had looked at me when I tried to tell him he'd do fine cutting into Syd's chest. Like he was the idiot this time.

"Why?" I asked. "Why will Lucy be OK? Did they take her off so they could set her up in a mansion with a lot of servants?"

Herb flushed a deep shade of pink. "Don't get cocky with me, Joey. Those b-----s stole every decent horse I owned, and several that I didn't, but that I'm responsible for just the same. I'll probably have to pay for them, too, god d---it."

"Is that what makes what happened to Lucy tolerable? That it's not going to cost you anything?"

He glared, but I didn't back down. Before the McCandles gang came to town, I probably would have.

"She's a whore, Joey," he said harshly. "They ain't gonna do anything to her that hasn't. . . ."

"I already heard that speech!" I shouted, and Herb reared back in surprise. "Happy Collins made it in the Palace last night, right before they kicked me out," I added, lowering my voice. I started to sniff and told myself it was because of the stink of fire. "Did you try to stop them?" I asked after a couple of minutes.

"We kept our heads down, like any sensible man would," Herb said.

After mulling that over in my mind for a while, I fixed him with a puzzled stare. "You let them burn down the Palace, and nearly the whole town? You let them kill two men and a woman, then kidnap another woman? You let them do all that, and you didn't do anything to stop it?"

"They were in a murdering mood, Joey. Syd got a couple of them before they shot him, but they were primed to kill anyone who got in their way after that."

"What about Lucy? What about protecting your town and your homes and your property?"

"Lucy will be fine, and the miners . . . well, they didn't have any family nearby that I'm aware of. The Hop Along will see that they get a decent burial. That's about all we can do."

I stared at Herb until his jaws began to tighten.

"You're too young to understand," he accused.

I waited for him to say more. When he didn't, I got to my feet. "Where's McCandles and his gang now?"

"They rode north out of town."

"With Lucy?"

"Yeah, with Lucy."

I crossed the street to the livery. Thankfully Herb didn't follow me.

Syd's gray, the one I called Hammerhead, was stilled stabled in the rear stall where I'm put him the day before. It didn't surprise me that McCandles's men had passed on the gelding. The gray was Roman-nosed and ewe-necked, and had a tail so thin it looked like it had been plucked. But looks don't always mean a lot when it comes to horses. Or people, I stewed. Anyway, there was a spunky horse underneath all that ugly, intelligent and deep-bottomed—a deep bottom being horse talk for an animal that could probably run all day if it had to. Or, in the gray's case, if I needed him to. Hammerhead was fast for a common horse. Nothing like a thoroughbred, or even Syd's palomino, but swift enough when put to the test. He was sure-footed over rocky terrain, too. In all the time I'd ridden him, I don't think I ever saw him trip over a clump of grass or a stone. Fact is, for what I had in mind, he was a near perfect mount.

I led the gray around to the shack where I was living and threw my rig on top and cinched it down. I still had a little food left over from the grub Syd had given me when I went out to bring in his cattle—some rice and beans, coffee, flour, dried fruit. There was even some jerky stuffed in a cloth sack for eating in the saddle. I shoved the food inside my saddlebags along with a tin billy for cooking and a cup and a spoon. I slid the Evans rifle into the scabbard, its butt jutting above the gray's right hip, then strapped my bedroll behind the cantle, fetched my heavy coat and gloves, and I was ready to ride.

I was just poking my shoe in the stirrup when Herb appeared at the livery's rear entrance.

"Joey!"

I swung up fast, planting my right foot firmly in the offside stirrup before Herb could reach my side. I reined around to put the gray's head between myself and the liveryman. "Don't try to stop me."

"Joey, I know you think you love her, but she isn't worth it. Trust me. I've known women like that ever since I was your age."

"Love's got nothing to do with it. It ain't right what they did to Lucy, but it ain't right what they did to this town, either. And it sure as h--- ain't right what they did to Syd. Maybe you don't mind letting them get away with it, but I do. I'm going after them."

"And do what?"

"Bring in Ian McCandles," I blurted, and I think I stunned

myself with that declaration as much as I did Herb. I hadn't known what I intended to do when I left Herb sitting on the boardwalk.

"What you're going to do is get your fool head blown off," Herb said. "Don't be a fool, Joey. Let someone else take care of McCandles and his gang."

"Who? You?"

Herb started to sputter a protest, but I cut him off.

"What if they come back someday and the Palace isn't here and all the whores are gone? Who do they take their mad out on then? You or Jim? Or Jim's wife? Would that be all right, if they took Marta with them the next time?"

Herb's face turned suddenly blotchy. "You know what, go on and get yourself killed, you ignorant colt. Nobody here will mourn your loss. H---, I doubt if anyone here will even know you're gone."

He was likely right about that, but his words didn't cut me the way he meant for them to. Fact is, I'd just about lost all my respect for Herb Smith. For Jim Sanders and Big Ed Farmer and all the rest of them. To h--- with them that wouldn't stand up for their own.

Pulling the gray's head around, I nudged his ribs with my heels and we jogged down the alley between the stable and the big corral where Syd's cattle were bawling at the smell of blood and death. On the street—Coalville only had one—I reined north into a stiffening breeze. I never looked back.

You're probably wondering why I'd leave town without checking in on Syd a final time, or making an effort to outfit myself properly. I should have, you know? I especially should have gone in to say good bye to Syd, whether he was conscious or not. Up until then, I don't reckon anyone had ever treated me better than Syd Hackett.

But seeing Syd a last time was just part of what I should have done that day. There was food to be had at both the Mercantile and the Hop On Inn, supplies I would need desperately in very short order, plus better firearms at the jail than my old Evans had ever been, weapons that would have been mine for the taking if I'd just done it.

I won't argue with anyone who wants to say that leaving like I did was pure foolishness, but I can see now that there was more to my decision than an urgency to bring in Ian McCandles. What I think I was trying to do was to escape the reality of everything that had happened over the last twelve hours. Not to mention what was going to happen as soon as the sun came up. I doubt if anyone, least of all Burt Newman, had any illusions about Syd's chances of recovering from surgery.

The sad fact is, I didn't want to be there when Syd passed away. That's the long and short of it right there. I didn't want to have to attend Syd's wake or funeral, or have to think about burying those two Hop Along miners and the whore, Ruby Davidson. I didn't want to have to help Adam Hoffman sort through the wreckage of his saloon, or to replace shattered windows and bullet-ruptured door panels. And I knew, down deep, that if I stayed for one, I would stay for them all. The truth is, I was running. Running out on the grief and the sense of failure I knew I'd have to contend with if I stayed. Come to think on it, maybe that's also why I didn't look back when I rode out of town.

The tracks left by McCandles's men were pretty easy to follow for the first hour or so. There wasn't much of a road going north. Most of Coalville's traffic originated from the south, and the majority of that came from Kelton. There were a few little mining communities up along the eastern slopes of the Black Pine Mountains, but nearly all of them outfitted out of Pocatello or Twin Falls. I couldn't figure out why McCandles was taking his men in that direction. After a few miles, I found out that he wasn't. On a high ridge cleaving down from the Black Pines, the trail veered abruptly to the west, and from then on their tracks became a lot harder to follow.

The weather had been cool and clear the day before, but the sun rose that morning into a sky layered with a thick, gray scud of clouds. The wind was brisk out of the northwest, and I rode quartering into it all day, the collar of my jacket pulled up high on my right side to protect that ear, my cap pulled down gingerly over the lump at the back of my cranium.

It was a rugged country I passed through. Lots of small cañons snaking down out of the Black Pine Mountains, the stony ridges reminding me of the exposed roots of a giant cottonwood. It would have been impossible for me to dog McCandles's trail the way I did if it hadn't been as large as it was. Even then, it was difficult—an occasional kicked-over stone or a gouged patch of earth where some horse had scrambled up or down a bank. If it had just been one or two riders, I doubt if I would have been able to keep up.

Toward the middle of the afternoon I spotted a shaded vortex hovering in the sky directly ahead of me, and my heart sank toward my belly. I kicked the gray into a lope, gritting my teeth at the increased throbbing in my head.

It took me an hour to reach the little flat where the buzzards were circling. I located the actual spot by the number of birds already on the ground, waddling back and forth like a crowd of egocentric old men. A couple of them stood on top of a low mound of rocks as if about to start pontificating on some subject near and dear to vultures everywhere, but they all flapped off when I rode up. Even from twenty yards away, I could smell death wiggling up out of its grave.

I looped the gray's reins over a clump of sagebrush to approach the final few yards on my own two wobbly feet. It wasn't the smell that had my stomach percolating and my head reel-ing, but the fear of what I was getting ready to uncover. I'll tell you what, I was just about in tears as I knelt there rolling stones off that grave.

Whoever had done the burying hadn't been particularly charitable in his labors. The grave was so shallow, I think if it hadn't been for the rocks stacked on top, the corpse's nose likely would have poked up out of the earth like an upside-down rudder. Swallowing the bile that kept creeping up the back of my throat, I brushed the loose soil away from the earthen remains.

My relief was immediate, although short-lived. It wasn't Lucy, and for that I was thankful enough to want to shout hallelujah to the heavens. I didn't, since I had no idea where McCandles and his boys might be, and I didn't want to draw attention to myself if they were close by. Then curiosity took over, and I continued clearing away the loose soil that dusted the outlaw's features.

Oh, I recognized him right off. One of McCandles's men whose name I'd never heard, a lantern-jawed bully who had been upstairs with the whores when I came back the second time with their grub. No, what was fueling my inquisitiveness was the cause of the man's demise. Herb had said that morning that Syd had killed two of the buggers before he himself had been brought down by the bandits' revolvers, but, unless the guy I was slowly exposing to the elements had been killed by one of his own, it was beginning to look as if Syd might have dropped three of them.

It took only a minute to uncover the upper half of the guy's body, and sure enough, there was a dirt- and blood-encrusted bandage wrapped tightly around his chest. That meant, in my opinion, that he'd probably been shot the night before, and that the gang had brought him along until he gave up the ghost out here in the middle of nowhere.

But there was something else I discovered. The guy didn't have on any of his outer clothes, just his long-handles, bandages, and a blue bandanna knotted loosely around his neck. I kept staring, unable to come up with a logical explanation for the outlaw's state of undress. It wasn't until a vulture—bald of head and curved of beak, eyes as moist and emotionless as freshly pitted cherry seeds—lumbered forward as if to ask if I was done yet, that I finally pushed to my feet.

Birds need to eat as much as wolves, and this long-jawed character at my feet would have provided the carrion eaters a hearty meal, but some smattering of decency prevented me from just riding away. Although irritated with myself for a delay I wasn't entirely sure was warranted, I began piling the stones back in place. I didn't take as much care about it as McCandles's men had—and Lord knew that hadn't been much—but I did replace enough rocks to keep the buzzards off. I figured like as not, if it came to it, that would be more than they would do for me.

I don't guess there's any need to relate everything that happened over the next few days. At least not in any detail. It was all pretty much the same after leaving the shallow grave. I do recall wondering more than once what McCandles and his men were up to. They seemed to ride in just about every direction of the compass at one point or another, and not so much as the lay of the land might dictate, either. I later figured out they were probably doing it to throw off pursuit, which was fairly laughable when you recall how Coalville's finest had cowered in the dark like a hatch of trembling rabbits. Except for horseflies and a fool-headed kid with a beat-up rifle riding a hammer-headed nag of an iron-gray horse, they needn't have worried about being chased.

The trail didn't get any easier to follow. I'd lose it from time to time, but always managed to pick it up again with a little back-and-forth searching. We were heading in a general westerly direction, and, when the gang finally gave up its wayward track and struck out for a low range of mountains on the distant horizon, I might have cheered if I hadn't been so tired.

The weather remained cold and cloudy the whole time, and not a day passed that I didn't see some far-off veil of angry blue bridging sky and earth with what I knew was rain. I was lucky, however, and never felt so much as a drop. By the time I guided my horse into the stumpy foothills that had been our destination all along, the clouds were finally starting to break apart. It didn't get any warmer, though. Not even when you could find a shaft of sunlight to ride through.

As the crow flies, I doubt if I was much over eighty miles from Coalville, but me and that gray had covered quite a bit more territory than that, what with all the back-and-forth riding we'd done following McCandles's trail. That part of southwestern Idaho was all new to me. I didn't know where I was for sure, just that we hadn't crossed any roads or seen any signs of civilization for two days. If it was a hide-out we were heading for, I decided McCandles had picked a perfect spot for it.

Although the trail didn't look any fresher then than it had on the day I'd left, I sensed I was coming to its end. I slowed the gray's pace accordingly, and spent more time eyeing the ridge lines for any hint of a look-out. The sun went down and the air turned frosty, my breath chuffing like a locomotive's chimney. The past few nights had found me searching for a place to spread my bedroll about now, but today I kept riding, veering off the trail only when full darkness closed in.

The terrain wasn't much different from what I was familiar with around the Black Pines—shallow cañons furred over with pines on their north-facing slopes, aspen groves looking like golden pelts from a distance sprouting at the mouths of the coulées that fingered down off the south-facing ridges.

It was into one of those side cañons that I eventually reined the gray, a sinuous course littered with crumbling boulders and thick patches of scrub, but it led me to the top in less than half an hour. Leaving the gray hitched to an aspen well below the skyline, I scrambled onto a rocky knoll that offered me a decent view of the surrounding country. I was looking for the telltale glow of a campfire to provide me with direction for the next day's travel, but all I saw was a deep black landscape under skies that were still largely overcast. I stayed up there an hour before the cold finally forced me down. Stepping into my saddle, I said: "Let's push on a spell."

I was speaking to Hammerhead, and it might sound odd to you that I did, but I'd discovered during my first trip into the high mountains with Syd's cattle that talking to your horse was an easy habit to fall into. Not too many years ago I had the opportunity to ride in a Packard Touring Car that had a radio in the front panel that could pick up any station within a fifty-mile radius, but back in the 1800s, when all we had for music were the wolves' howls and the coyotes' yips, a horse made a mighty fine companion.

I rode all night, staying mostly to the ridge tops where I could keep an eye on the buckling hills. I was still hoping to catch the glimmer of a distant campfire, but all I ended up with was a sore butt. By the time dawn rolled up over the horizon, my eyes were feeling like they had been lubricated with sand. The headache that had started to fade after my second day on the trail was creeping back, too, like thumbs pressed steadily against the backs of my eyes.

With the morning light, I reined into some aspens. I danged near hit the ground when I dismounted, my legs were so numb. A little spring-fed stream cutting through the center of the trees and tall, summer-cured grass along its banks offered all the essentials a horse might need for a day on the end of a picket rope. After seeing to the gray, I unfurled my bedroll and wiggled inside without any thought of breakfast. I was asleep almost before I got my toes tucked in, and I don't believe I moved a muscle until midafternoon, when the gray's loud nicker cracked the hard shell of my slumber.

I might have been sound asleep, but I was out of my blankets in a flash and at the gray's side in the next instant. The gelding's head was up, its ears perked toward the ridge we'd come off of at first light. I grabbed his soft nose, ready to give it a hard squeeze and a twist if he tried to call out a second time. Although I couldn't hear anything myself, I knew that didn't mean much. A horse's sense of just about everything—including, I've come to believe, *common*—is far superior to a human's, and I wasn't going to risk my neck thinking that just because I didn't see or hear or smell anything out of the ordinary, that there wasn't anything there.

Of course, anything is exactly what it could have been. I was hunting Ian McCandles, but these mountains, as piddling as they might seem compared to the Tetons or the Sawtooths, were filled with elk and deer and cougars and bears and who knows what else. The Indians tell of a hairy, ape-like creature standing eight or nine feet tall that wanders the more remote regions of the West, stories that still give me the willies today, and that I always tried real hard not to think about back then.

After twenty minutes or so, the gray seemed to lose interest in whatever had caught his attention. I let him return to his grazing, but there was no way I was going back to bed after that. My nerves were frazzled, so, grabbing my rifle, I made my way to the top of the ridge, dropping to my belly to crawl the last few yards.

Easing inside some rabbitbrush to camouflage my outline, I scanned the valley below me. When I spotted a trio of cow elk coming out of the tall pines across the way, just about every

muscle in my body twitched. I studied the dark stand of trees
carefully, and although I didn't see anything ominous, I could
tell by the way the cows were traveling—trotting swiftly
downhill, then stopping every thirty to forty yards to throw a
quick look behind them—that something had them spooked.
Shinnying back off the ridge, I returned to the aspens to saddle
my horse.

I circled well to the east of where the elk had come out of the
timber, then made my way back toward them on foot, keeping
inside the cover of pines and leading the gray by the reins, the
Evans held firmly in my right hand. Finding the prints of the
three elk wasn't difficult in the thick carpet of pine needles.
Turning onto their trail, I backtracked toward the next valley
over. At the top of the ridge I paused to study the wide valley
below me. It didn't take long to discover what had frightened
the cows. Not half a mile upcañon lay the carcass of a freshly
skinned bull elk. With my heart thumping in my ears, I swung a
leg over my saddle and rode on down.

Whoever had butchered the elk—it was a forked horn, I saw
when I got up closer—had long since departed. He'd sure
enough had plenty of time for it, what with the roundabout way
I'd taken coming in. I wondered if it was the hunter's shot that
had spooked the gray earlier. Keeping to my saddle, I circled
the slaughtered animal from some yards away. Most of the meat
had been taken, telling me that whoever had harvested this feast
likely had more than a few mouths to feed.

I believe I already mentioned this, but I'll say it again. There
had been nine hardcases who rode into Coalville on the evening
I returned from the Black Pines with Syd's Herefords. Ian Mc-
Candles, who had already been there a few days, made it an
even ten. Syd had reduced that number by three when the lights
went out in the Palace and the shooting started—testimony, I
might add, to the effectiveness of a sawed-off scatter-gun at

close range. That left seven, plus Lucy if she was still alive. I figured that many people would make quick work of a young bull elk, especially if they planned to settle in for a spell.

The trail leading away from the forked horn angled southwest, toward a hogback ridge covered in scattered piñon and jutting boulders. There were two sets of prints, one probably carrying the shooter, the second likely packing the choicer cuts of elk. Although the shooter hadn't made any effort to hide his tracks, it was a rugged country, and somewhere along the way I lost his sign. I doubled back to explore a couple of side gulches, but didn't have any luck. It was as if both horses and hunter had suddenly taken wing.

Not knowing what else to do, I continued on toward the hogback. I found a long-established deer trail leading over the top, but there were no fresh tracks in its middle, neither horse nor horned. Pulling up to ruminate on it, I finally came to the conclusion that the guy I'd been following had either veered off in another direction, or that he'd spotted me and was laying in wait somewhere nearby.

As soon as that second scenario popped into my mind, my scalp started to crawl like it was home to one of the largest flea circuses ever to tour the United States. I swear my eyes were darting in about half a dozen different directions at once. You think that can't be done, but if you ever get scared enough, you'll soon figure out what I'm talking about.

It occurred to me that if I was being watched, I needed to get the h--- off of that trail just as fast as I could. Yanking the gray around, I drove my heels into his ribs. Startled by the harshness of the kick, the gelding took off like a Kentucky Derby winner, faster than even I'd intended, but that was all right as far as I was concerned. I gave him all the rein he needed, and just concentrated on hanging on.

After about a mile, when the gray began to slow down, I

reined into a stand of scrawny pines and swung to the ground. Leaving the horse secured in the trees, I snuck back for a look-see, but only my own settling dust disturbed the tranquility of the narrow valley. White clouds, rather than the dingy gray ones that had shaded me all the way from Coalville, dotted the blue sky, and birds flitted from limb to limb, doing whatever it is that birds do. Their songs, along with the wind in the pines, was a comfort to listen to, and I sank to the ground with my back to a scaly trunk, the Evans cradled in my lap. Then a gunshot rang out, the bullet passing. . . .

SESSION FOUR

That machine picks some awkward moments to run out of disc. I guess it doesn't matter as long as it records the whole story, but it's a distraction in my opinion. I like the pen and paper method better myself.

So anyway, there was that gunshot where the bullet passed just over my head, and I figured sure as Hades I'd been spotted. I dived for the roots on the far side of that pine and pulled the Evans close. Rolling onto my back, I levered a round into the chamber. Meanwhile, nothing else happened, and, when I sneaked a peek around the tree trunk, there wasn't a soul to be seen.

The gray stood rigidly, its head thrown high, ears cocked to the south. Following the direction of its gaze revealed just more of the same—trees and rocks and low brush. Sucking in a deep breath, I pressed the tiny knob in front of the Evans' trigger to lock the hammer on safety.

An Evans is an uncommon little firearm. Technically, with its short barrel and the band holding it to the fore stock, mine isn't even a rifle. It's a carbine. But I'm going to call it a rifle because that's what I've always called it.

The Evans doesn't have a normal hammer, similar to the side hammer on a Sharps or Spencer; nor does it have a top-mounted hammer like a Winchester, although you work the lever just like you do on a Winnie. No, the Evans' hammer is under the receiver, just in front of the trigger guard. Spent brass is expelled through a slot on the right side of the action.

What makes the Evans even more unique is its magazine. Like the Spencer of Civil War days, the Evans loads through a port drilled through the butt. Point the muzzle toward the ground and drop in a cartridge, then lever it forward along the helix-shaped magazine—imagine a spiral staircase leading down—before dropping in a second round. Do that until the gun is fully loaded, which is going to take a while because the Evans has a voracious appetite for ammunition, thanks to its oddly shaped magazine. The Spencer holds seven rounds loaded straight down the stock. The Evans carries twenty-eight cartridges wrapped around its center pole—a lot more ammunition, but also several extra pounds of weight in the butt.

The Evans isn't a powerful weapon by any stretch of the imagination. It shoots a .44 cartridge only slightly longer and more potent than the .44-40 Winchester round that was so popular in those days, although it lacked the slight bottleneck shape that makes a .44-40 so danged frustrating to reload. I don't know what kind of accuracy a person could expect from a new Evans, but mine left a lot to be desired, more than likely because whoever had shortened the barrel had gotten the muzzle a tad off of ninety degrees. At one hundred yards, it printed groups at least a foot in diameter, which is poor shooting in my book. Take that cougar I'd dispatched after it killed several of Syd's calves. You can bet I made sure I was under fifty yards when I fired my first round. Then I shot it a second time from about ten yards away to be certain it was dead.

Anyway, I figured you ought to know what I was up against as far as firepower was concerned, not just what McCandles and his men carried, but my own limitations. Like I said earlier, I'd been a fool to ride out of Coalville without making sure I was adequately armed, especially considering how many firearms there had been at my disposal in the sheriff's office. I could have borrowed any one of them if I'd been thinking clearly. But remember, too, that I'd just seen Syd looking like death warmed over, even before Burt started cutting on him. Then I'd learned that Lucy had been abducted and several others killed while the people I'd always thought were so special, so d---ed high and mighty that their very words were law, had done nothing to prevent it.

That's something that has haunted me my entire life, the way those townsfolk didn't do anything to stop McCandles and his boys, or to back up Syd when he attempted to retrieve their stolen horses. About ten or fifteen years ago I was attending a lecture down at the Masonic Hall, and they had a speaker who elaborated on paradigms, those so-called truths that a person accepts as absolute—such as the sky being blue or that the sun comes up in the east. I think that's what got knocked out of kilter for me that night in Coalville. It was a major paradigm shift, and it has colored the way I look at the world ever since.

But that's enough of that. You didn't come here to record an old man's opinions on what's wrong with society. You want to hear about my heroic efforts to rescue the fair damsel, Lucy Lytle, and to bring a murderer to justice.

Well, like I said when you first contacted me, you're going to be almighty disappointed when the whole story is laid out bare for everyone to see.

Back behind that pine tree, I probably waited a good twenty minutes for something to happen. I kept expecting a barrage of bullets to come my way at any minute, but nothing else interrupted the day's serenity, and after a while the gray lowered its head to nibble at some grass. Seeing that, I began to relax, too. Someone might put a successful sneak on me without much effort, but I knew they'd never slip up on the gray.

Taking a firm grip on my rifle, I edged out to where I had a better view to the south. There was a low rise in front of me covered in pines, but with plenty of rocks and scrub to hide in. Leaving the gray tethered, I made my way to the top.

What I saw on the other side of that rise nearly caused my jaw to bounce off the ground. D---ed if it wasn't a little settlement. It might have been crude enough to make Coalville look like a bustling metropolis, but, as soon as I saw it, I knew what I'd found. For several years people had been talking about an outlaw hide-out in the Owyhee country. Not right on the river itself—it would have been too easily found there—but somewhere within the Owyhee's sprawling drainage.

You've heard of Robbers' Roost and Hole in the Wall? They called this place Horse Thieves' Gulch, and, judging from the sizeable herd of ponies I saw grazing on the rich autumn grass across the way, I figured it had been aptly named.

What I was looking at wasn't so much a gulch as a wide, shallow valley. A stream several feet in width wound down its middle, and a fair-size log building stood on the west bank, its roof shingled in sod, tall grass, and weeds. Smaller lodgings—a regular little burg of shacks, cabins, and canvas lean-tos—had sprung up around it, and a narrow, steep-sided cañon straight across from me had a fence built across both ends where I suspected they penned the saddle stock at night.

A few of the sturdier buildings had small corrals tacked on behind them, but most of the structures looked like a good strong wind might blow them down. From what I'd heard in Coalville, I reckoned that biggest building to be a combination trading post and saloon run by an ex-Confederate named Danson.

Although folks talked about Horse Thieves' Gulch all the time, I'd never known anyone to say they had actually seen the place. I figured I was probably the first from Coalville to do so.

Crawling under a bush, I settled down to study the place more thoroughly. There were a few people about, even some women and kids and dogs, but it was overall a grungy-looking spread. Deer and elk hides had been tossed willy-nilly, each one sporting its own tiny cloud of blowflies, and sun-bleached bones were scattered everywhere. Smoke rose from several of the buildings, and an elderly Indian woman was standing next to a large iron kettle hanging over a low fire in front of the trading post. Yet for all that, the town looked basically deserted, a couple of the brush shelters already starting to collapse in on themselves.

I might as well tell you now that I never did learn who had fired that shot, or why. I guess in a community like Horse Thieves' Gulch, it could have been just about anyone, and for any reason. I was happy enough just to know that I hadn't been the intended target.

I studied the lay of the land carefully to fix it in my mind, having already decided that I would slip in after dark for a closer look. I figured it was a good bet that McCandles and Lucy were down there somewhere. As it turned out, they were, and I didn't have to go looking for them, either.

It was well into the gloaming when activity began to pick up. A kid rode out on horseback to bring in the horses, and a door to a squatty log cabin next to the creek swung open to spill lamplight onto the dirt. A woman stepped out, short and chunky and kind of pretty in a full-length red skirt, although it was the frilly camisole she wore up top that caught my teen-age attention. Her white shoulders seemed to glow in the dusky light. She had wavy red hair that came down just far enough to cover her neck in back, and apple-like cheeks that looked buffed from the wind. I would later learn that the red in her cheeks was a skin condition she abhorred, but was unable to cover up due to a lack of proper make-up, the gulch being so far off the beaten path that powder and paint—the feminine kind, at any rate—was practically unheard of.

She stood in the cabin's door for several minutes watching the kid gather the horses, then, apparently tiring of the show, she twisted at the waist to call into the cabin. My head popped up several inches when Lucy came outside to stand beside her.

Remember that dead man I'd come across my first day out, and how he'd been stripped down to his long-handles? Now I knew why. Lucy was wearing his clothes, and it was probably a smart move, considering the silky outfit she'd been wearing that night in the Palace.

The redhead spoke, then pointed out a brush privy set off to one side. Lucy headed for it like she'd been needing it for a while. The redhead waited at the door, and, when Lucy came back, they both walked down to the creek, where Lucy filled a wooden bucket with water that she carried back to the cabin. Both women went inside, the redhead slamming the door shut with a bang that reached all the up to where I was stretched out in the shadows.

I exhaled loudly, not even aware that I had been hoarding my breath. I tried to make sense of what I'd seen. The redhead had clearly been the boss, but it hadn't looked like Lucy was being guarded too closely. Maybe, I thought, because there was no place for her to go even if she could have gotten away.

I watched the kid haze the horses into the side cañon. With the remuda inside, he swung down and latched the gate, then stripped the tack from his own mount and turned it loose. He took his gear to a small arbor nearby and shoved it inside, then made his way to the trading post. The Indian woman had already gone inside with her kettle of food, and the kids and dogs had disappeared. A peaceful silence fell over the community. Like it was just a normal town.

With full dark, I scuttled back from the rim and returned to the gray. "She's there, boy," I told the horse, "and I'll bet you a nickel's worth of oats that Ian McCandles is somewhere close by, too."

Actually I figured it was a pretty good bet McCandles was in the trading post, which, if it was anything like most of the other establishments of its kind that I've seen over the years, would have a bar for drinking and tables for gambling. If that was the case, then sooner or later he'd head over to the redhead's cabin to claim his prize. It never occurred to me that he might have already done so, or that Lucy might not even be his to claim. H---, for all I knew, it might have been another member of the gang who had kidnapped her.

I checked the gray's cinch, then led the horse out of the pines and stepped into the saddle, laying the Evans across the pommel in front of me where it would be quick to shoulder. I knew where I wanted to go and what I needed to do in order to rescue Lucy and arrest McCandles, and I was strangely eager to get the ball rolling.

It took me an hour to circle the ridge so that I could approach the gulch from downwind. I was still a few hundred yards shy of the nearest building when I dismounted and led my horse into a grove of quaking aspen. On foot, I made my way toward the little town. Coming up behind a dark shanty, I put an ear to one of the broader cracks in the wall. Not hearing anything that would suggest it was occupied, I eased around the corner and I slipped inside.

Another wide gap in the opposite wall offered me my best view yet of the gulch. The cabin where they were keeping Lucy was less than fifty yards away. As with the front, there were no windows in back, but there was lamplight squirting out from between the logs where the chinking had fallen away, like butter from a sandwich.

Spotting a small corral behind the cabin, I felt like whooping when I spied Syd's palomino standing hip-shot under a lean-to with a couple of other horses. There was even a saddle sitting on its horn to one side, bridle and pad draped over the upright skirting.

There were at least three windows in the trading post that I could see from here, and the front door had been thrown open in spite of the cold. From my place in the shanty I couldn't see anyone inside, but I could hear the soft babble of voices. Letting my gaze drift over the ramshackle community, I suddenly stiffened. A lone rifleman sat on a tree stump maybe twenty yards in front of the trading post. At first I thought he was just lollygagging, but after a few minutes I realized he was watching the main trail that wound up from the lowlands to the north.

I hadn't counted on a look-out, and I pulled back from the gap to think. It occurred to me that there had probably been someone there all day, and that, like the horses behind the cabin, I just hadn't spotted him from my position on the ridge.

My hopes that had soared so high when I spotted the palomino were now nestled around my ankles like a pair of trousers several sizes too large. The guard wasn't so far away that I couldn't have dropped him if I wanted to, but even a green kid like me knew better than to raise a ruckus in that kind of a situation. Just one shot, and I could imagine Danson's post spilling hardcases like beans out of a ripped sack.

I stood there with my back pressed against the wall for several minutes before a plan began to take shape in my mind. It would be risky as h--- and nothing much for fancy, but maybe it would work. I hoped it would work.

Shifting the Evans to my left hand, I tiptoed out the door and around the far side. From here, the look-out's back was to me, the whole of the gulch spread out before the both of us. He was rolling a cigarette, sitting with one heel cocked up on the lip of the stump, his attention focused on the paper and tobacco in front of him. Real cautious, I shortened the distance between us, planting each foot with as much care as if I were walking barefoot through broken glass. As I inched closer, I also kept an eye on the ground, and it didn't take long to collect a pocketful of fist-size stones.

I'd been eating pretty regularly the last few years because of Syd and all the oddball chores he kept coming up with for me to do. As tight-fisted as he was, he didn't often pay me in cash, but he'd tell me to run on over to the Hop On Inn and have Jim fix me a meal that I'd eat on his tab, which, of course, the town paid for. But Jim never hesitated and I never abused the privilege of having a decent supper on a more or less steady basis, and things had worked out fairly well.

Before Syd came along, though, my belly had been through some lean times. As a consequence, I had become something of a street rat, filching grub wherever I could find it, scrounging around in the town dump for food and clothes, even stealing eggs and garden truck when the opportunity presented itself. And I got to be something of an expert at knocking over rabbits with rocks. A rabbit makes a nice little meal for a hungry kid, especially when I could steal some salt or pepper for seasoning. Lord knew there was no shortage of rabbits in those days, both jacks and cottontails. If I could get within thirty feet of a bunny with a good smooth rock and a clear shot, I'd probably eat that night. I was good at it, and, as I snuck up on that look-out occupied with his cigarette that didn't want to stay sealed, I was hoping the skill hadn't deserted me.

About twenty paces shy of the *hombre*'s back, I quietly sat my rifle aside and wound up for the pitch. I don't know, maybe I was nervous, or maybe it was the poor light—just freckling stars and the moon over my left shoulder—but I missed him clean. The guy's head jerked up as the rock sailed past his ear, but when it hit the dirt close to the big corral he didn't pay it any mind. Sounded too much like a horse stomping its hoof, I guess.

Cursing under my breath, I pulled another stone from my pocket. The guy was standing now, staring down the gulch away from me. He knew something was up, but hadn't yet figured out what it was. I was going to be chin-deep in dung if I missed him a second time.

I wound up in my best Dizzy Dean form, paused just a moment to eye my shadowy target—right under and a little back of where I pictured his left ear to be—then let 'er fly.

My pitch was true, and that rock made an impressive thump when it struck the fellow's head. The way he fell reminded me of the blow I'd taken to my own skull, back in Coalville, and I knew he'd wake up tomorrow with a h--- of a headache.

Snatching up my rifle, I hurried over there quick as a squirrel to roll him onto his back. I didn't recognize him, which was a relief, since I didn't want to have to haul him back to Coalville along with McCandles. I would have attempted it, though, had he been one of the gang.

It was right about then that something happened that I've recalled many times over the years. Staring down at the guy's slack features, it dawned on me what I was about to do.

My original goal had always been to bring in Ian McCandles and, if possible, rescue Lucy Lytle. Sure, I'd fantasized along the way about hauling the whole bunch back to Coalville, their hands tied behind their backs, their grimy faces sagging in defeat. Yet even as I pictured it in my mind, I knew in my heart it wouldn't be possible. Not for a posse of marshals, and sure as Hades not for a seventeen-year-old kid on a hammer-headed gray gelding.

No, I'd decided early on that I'd have to settle for rescuing Lucy and making a citizen's arrest of McCandles. But now that I was actually in the midst of it, standing above an unconscious outlaw with a cocked rifle in my hands, a trading post populated with who knew how many hardcases not thirty yards away, the enormity of my goal just exploded through me. I must have stood there frozen under the weight of my own arrogance for a full minute before my paralysis finally broke with the realization that I wasn't just thinking about it any more, I was *doing* it. I was slaying a dragon so that I could rescue a damsel in distress.

And d---ed if I wasn't doing it on ol' Hammerhead.

I think I was actually trembling from a rush of adrenaline when I reached down to grab a handful of the guy's collar. I dragged him into the shanty from where I'd first spied him, then used his own belt to tie his arms behind his back. I shoved his neck rag into his mouth to keep him from hollering if he came around too soon, then tossed his rifle and revolver into the weeds out back where they wouldn't be easily found.

I know, I know. Everything I've already said about leaving Coalville without decent weapons, and what's the first thing I do when I get my hands on some? I pitched them out like yesterday's potato peelings. I wasn't thinking. That's the long and short of it right there.

Anyway, with the look-out trussed up and out of my hair, I went back to the cabin where I'd seen Lucy earlier. A crack between a couple of the logs offered me a full view of the inside. The chunky redhead with the apple cheeks was there, although she didn't look nearly so fetching up close. She was bent over a skillet balanced on some rocks in the fireplace, her back to Lucy, who was sitting alone at a crudely built table, a mournful expression dragging at her features.

I stepped away from the cabin and crawled through the rails of the small corral. I was lucky that Syd's palomino recognized me and didn't raise a fuss, and because he accepted me, the other horses did, too. The saddle and bridle I'd seen earlier were just outside the gate, and I made quick work of getting everything cinched down. Then I made a smart decision for a change. I put halters and lead ropes on the other two horses, a bay and a sorrel, and hitched them alongside the palomino.

With the horses ready, I returned to the cabin. Everything was as before except that the redhead had fetched up a little three-legged stool that she was sitting on, while Lucy fiddled at the table with a knife like she was carving her initials into the wood.

As soundlessly as I could, I worked my way around to the front of the cabin. The door was a slab-wood affair on leather hinges, sundered vertically with strips of light from inside. Halting to one side, I tapped softly on the pine planks. After a moment's silence, the redhead shouted: "Who the blank is it?"

Only the word she used wasn't *blank*. It was something a heck of a lot worse, and that I'm not going to repeat here. Let's just say she was a coarse old broad with a vocabulary both extensive and creative when it came to profanity—and I say that having grown up in a rough-hewn coal mining community.

I was so taken aback by her uncouth response that I didn't immediately know how to answer. Fortunately I didn't have to. I heard a piece of furniture hit the wall—the three-legged stool, I would learn—then the door flew open and the redhead stepped into the jamb. She glared at me like she was contemplating which to rip out first, my heart or my throat.

"Who the blank are you?" she demanded.

"Joey!" Lucy gasped, and the redhead swung partway around to scowl at her.

"You know this runt?"

That was all the opening I needed. I slipped sideways into the cabin, making an extra effort not to brush up against anything feminine.

"Whoa, buster," the redhead said, putting a hand against my chest and pinning me to the door frame. "I didn't say you could come in."

I showed her the business end of my rifle, but she just swatted it aside like most of us would a fly on a supper plate.

"Get that thing outta my face," she growled, then turned to Lucy. "This one of Ian's new men?"

Lucy hesitated like she didn't know what to say. Me, I was starting to feel real uncomfortable, standing there in the light of a coal-oil lamp with Danson's trading post so close. I pushed inside and elbowed the door closed.

"Buster . . . ," the redhead started to say, but I'd gotten my voice back by then and didn't let her finish.

"Get back," I ordered with all the authority I could muster.

She narrowed her eyes suspiciously, but complied. "What do you want?"

"I came to rescue Lucy."

Lucy jumped up to her feet, her eyes brightening. "Who else is out there?"

"No one. It's just me."

She stared incomprehensibly for a moment. Then her expression crumbled and she collapsed back onto the bench where she had been sitting.

The redhead snorted. "Some knight in shining armor you are," she said.

I looked from her to Lucy and back again, and for a moment my confidence withered. Then I shook my head and said: "I'm all she's got, and the only one who came. I'm taking her home."

"Joey," Lucy said, "you can't rescue me. Ian'll kill you if you try."

"He'll likely kill you anyway, once he learns you're here," the redhead said.

"Leave him be, Della," Lucy said.

I looked at the redhead. "Wild Horse Della?"

She laughed. No, that's not quite right. Wild Horse Della Wilson never really laughed in all the time I knew her. Not in the traditional sense. It was more of a cackle, like something you'd expect from a witch standing over her cauldron. There was meanness in the sound, but never any humor that I heard. Della wasn't all that old when I knew her, but she was, let's just say, *experienced* in the ways of hired love. And with the rattly inflection of a heavy smoker, she sounded old.

"Heard of me, have you?" she asked.

I nodded. Della was famous for certain tricks of a kind I'd never quite known whether or not to believe. Not just that a woman would do them, but that a woman could do them. Let's leave it at that.

"What are you doing out here?" I asked.

"I was shanghaied, same as your little birdy over there." Then she asked me what I was doing out there, but I won't elaborate on her choice of words. In fact, from here on out, I'll pretend she was as polite as a choir girl, so long as you understand that if I repeated every loutish remark or crude expletive she uttered, your recordings will be half again as long as they're already going to be.

Anyway, I repeated my goal of rescuing Lucy, then added that I intended to take Ian McCandles back, as well.

"That's a hoot," Della said. "He'll pop your head like a fat tick when he gets back."

I looked at Lucy. "Is he coming back?"

She nodded. "He's been at Danson's all afternoon, but Della expects him back anytime now."

"Ian's a poor poker player when he's drunk, and he was well on his way when I took him his lunch," Della said. "Yeah, he'll be back soon enough. I was just fixing him some supper."

I pointed my rifle at her. "Go on about your business, then. I'll wait."

"Joey, don't do this," Lucy said. "Get out of here while you can."

Della returned to the fireplace, righting her stool and plunking herself down on top of it. I stepped to one side so that I'd be behind the door when it opened.

"Joey?"

"No, I'm not leaving without McCandles."

"Why? Because he killed Syd?"

Lucy's words struck me hard. The truth was, Syd hadn't been dead when I left Coalville, and even though I figured he was by now, hearing someone else say it gave it a finality I hadn't anticipated.

"Joey, please."

I just shook my head. I'd come too far to ride away now.

After a bit, Della dished up a plate of beans and beef, or slow elk, as she called it. The term was something of a joke among cattle rustlers and homesteaders of the day, who saw nothing wrong in butchering another man's beeves for their own table. Ask them what they were eating and they'd grin real smug and say it was a slow elk they'd shot, but everyone knew what they meant.

I dug in like I was starving, which, as most folks know, is the typical appetite of seventeen-year-old boys everywhere. It's part of the growing process, I guess, but after being out in the windy cold for so long, afraid to build a fire for warmth or food, subsisting on tough jerky and dried fruit, I was hungry enough to eat just about any kind of meat thrown in front of me—slow, fast, or stewed.

I ate my share and more, and Della was eyeing me with considerable vexation by the time I swiped the skillet clean with the last biscuit.

"Christ, boy, I once ate with a cavalry detachment that didn't put away as much food as you just did."

"I was hungry."

"I'm just glad I don't have to foot the bill for your nightly fare. I doubt a woman could whore fast enough to buy all the grub you'd suck down."

She was an ornery woman, and not just in her manner. She was truly mean-spirited, but I don't think it was lost upon her that I'd kept the Evans by my side while I ate, and never took my eyes off her longer than it took to stab another piece of meat with my fork.

Lucy washed the dishes afterward, while Della returned to her three-legged stool in front of the fireplace to smoke a cigar. She would glance at me every once in a while and chuckle like she was envisioning something funny. I knew she was trying to irritate me, or maybe just undermine my confidence, but I was too wound up to let her tactics get to me. I had my own visions of what might happen if I screwed up.

It was probably closing in on midnight when I heard someone approaching the cabin. Della had long since finished her smoke and taken to bed. Lucy was still sitting at the table, but with her head resting on her folded arms; she was snoring gently. I got to my feet and nervously moved behind the door. What I heard from outside was shuffling footsteps and a slurred tune sung off-key—a ditty I'd never heard before, but which I've never forgotten.

> *When I was a little bitty baby,*
> *Just up off the floor,*
> *My Mama said these words to me, she said:*
> *"Son, someday you'll grow up be a bore."*
>
> *Now I love my Mama,*
> *About as much as any boy can,*
> *But when she said those words to me,*
> *I smacked her in the face with a frying pan.*
>
> *Oh, Mama, flat-faced Mama,*
> *Look what you made me do.*

Oh, Mama, flat-faced Mama,
You look like the bottom of my shoe.

You can probably figure out for yourself why the song never caught on.

As the voice drew closer and louder, Lucy lifted her head and Della raised up in her blankets. Giving me a broad wink, Della said: "Here's your chance to be a real man, buster. Think you're up to it?"

I told her to shut her mouth, then motioned for Lucy to get out of the way, but she just scowled and shook her head, and Della laughed. Then the door swung inward and Ian McCandles stumbled inside. As soon as he did, I kicked the door shut and jammed the muzzle of my rifle into the pit of his stomach. I was just about to tell him to throw up his hands and surrender when he knocked the barrel aside and punched me in the face.

I likely have McCandles's drunkenness to thank for the ineptitude of his swing. Had he had his wits about him, I probably would have been murdered on the spot. As it was, I reeled backward to collide with the basin of dirty water Lucy had used to wash the supper dishes. I lost my balance and fell, the basin coming down with me to soak my whole right side with greasy dish water.

"Don't I know you?" McCandles asked, drawing his revolver.

I searched frantically for my dropped rifle but couldn't find it anywhere.

"Yeah, you're that kid from Coalville, ain't cha?" he said. "The one who brought us our supper."

He leveled his nickeled Colt at my heart, and I figured I was dead meat for sure. Likely I would have been if not for Lucy. She said, sweet as a fresh-baked blueberry pie: "Ian."

The bandit never took his eyes off of me, but he smiled at her voice, and his finger paused on the trigger. "What can I do for you, darlin'?" he asked. "After you clean up the mess this kid is gonna leave behind when I blow his god-d---ed head. . . ."

I heard a loud whack, and Ian's eyes first widened in surprise, then slowly rolled back toward his skull as if he wanted to assess the damage from the inside. He dropped to his knees, and I figured he might still pull the trigger—the muzzle hadn't wavered off my chest—but then his fingers loosened rather than tightened and the revolver tumbled to the floor. Ian swayed above it a moment longer, then plopped forward across my legs.

Standing behind him with a cast-iron skillet clutched like a baseball bat in both hands, Lucy stared at the outlaw's prostrate form. When she was sure he was out cold, she turned her attention to me.

"You *idiot*," she hissed. "You *never* give a man like Ian Mc-Candles an even break. You kill him on the spot or club him if he isn't looking, but you don't ever stand that close to a madman and expect him to just wait there while you make up your mind what to do."

It was sound advice, and she had a lot more to offer in that vein, her language growing coarser as she went on. Della was staying out of it, perched on the edge of her bunk with an expression of admiration on her face for Lucy's rapid-fire condemnations. I'd learn later that Lucy had been pretty subdued since her arrival at Horse Thieves' Gulch, but she was more than making up for it now. When I saw that she wasn't going to let up anytime soon, I pulled my legs out from under the outlaw and rose to my feet. Now that I wasn't desperate for it, I spotted the Evans right off. I grabbed that and Ian's Colt before I did anything else. Lucy was still going strong when I said: "Hush, now, and get some rope."

"What? Why?"

"So I can tie him up."

"You don't need to tie him up." She picked up the knife that she'd been using earlier to carve on the table and handed it to me. "Kill him."

Della erupted into laughter. "He's not going to knife the man, honey. He's going to take him back to civilization so that the law can hang him proper-like. Ain't that right, bub?"

"Get some rope," I told Lucy.

Although she shook her head as if the idea disgusted her, she nevertheless brought down a coil of half-inch hemp and tossed it on the table. "You're just going to get yourself killed, Joey."

I handed her the knife. "Cut off enough to tie his hands and feet."

She hesitated only a moment, then measured out what she thought I'd need and sliced off two equal lengths. From her bunk, Della said: "You really think you've got what it takes to haul this tiger back to civilization?"

"I intend to try."

The older woman eyed me speculatively for a second or two, then said: "Take me with you."

I looked at her in surprise.

"Take me with you, kid. It never was my intent to come out here in the first place. Danson bribed me with promises of gold and silver, but all the local owlhoots figure I ain't nothing but public property now."

Della's request had caught me off guard, but I didn't see how I could turn her down. And I did have that extra horse out back that she could ride. She'd have to straddle it bareback, though, there being no sign of another saddle anywhere in the cabin.

"You wouldn't leave a poor, helpless gal alone out here with this bunch of wild coyotes, would you?" Della persisted.

I think the last thing Wild Horse Della Wilson ever reminded me of was a helpless female, but she was right about one thing. I couldn't leave her behind. Not if she wanted to come with us.

"All right. Grab some food and blankets and whatever else you think we'll need. Lucy, help me tie up this jasper. The way you popped him, he might not come around for a few hours, and I want to be well down the road before he does."

FROM THE
Pocatello Democrat
DECEMBER 4, 1905
"IDAHO BY-WAYS"
BY COLUMNIST
MAXWELL TIERNEY

It has long been rumored that Idaho was once home to an outlaw's enclave every bit as wicked as Robbers' Roost in Utah or the infamous Hole in the Wall of Wyoming fame. As many of you know, it has been my ambition for a number of years to uncover the truth of this "tale that refuses to die," and it now appears that my efforts have "borne fruit," so to speak.

It was my pleasure recently to make the acquaintance of one Ernesto "Ernie" Vasquez, of Oakley. Ernie is one of that indomitable breed of men who haunt our fair state's more remote vales and peaks as a shepherd of the flock, though not in a religious sense. Mr. Vasquez herds sheep, and has since he was little more than a toddler, stumbling along with boyish delight after his father, the senior Ernesto. (Or is that *"Señor"* Ernesto, as both father and offspring bear the marked resemblance of their native Mexico?)

Ernie's name was presented to me by loyal Oakley reader Mrs. Elizabeth H. Fairchild, who was made aware of my interest in Idaho's rendition of a "viper's nest of dishonesty" by my mention of the subject in last October's bi-weekly column: "Does History Lie, or Merely Fib?"

Mrs. Fairchild mentioned in her rambling note a story told to her by her husband's handyman, the self-same Ernesto Vasquez, on one of his visits to render a stack of wood into manageable stove-length pieces. Rest assured, dear reader, that I made no half-hearted effort to extract myself from the confines of my cluttered office, with its cacophony of clattering typewriters and clanging telephones, and hastened forthwith to the quaint burg of one Oakley, Idaho.

I found Ernie gainfully employed at a task not unfamiliar to many of us, that is, the chopping of firewood for winter's consumption. In this particular instance, it was for the local grocery, for which we hope he was justly rewarded. I have chopped many a "rick" of firewood in my day, and I find nothing enviable in Mr. Vasquez's employment.

The story Ernie told, with no small amount of "prodding" and "exhortation" on my part, proved to be one of utter fascination not only to myself, but, I am certain, to you.

According to Mr. Vasquez, he was but a mere lad in the summer of 1884 or 1885, when he was hired by one Robert Walker, of the now dismantled Walker and Gaines Wool and Garment Corporation. Esquires Walker and Gaines had purchased as a source of raw material for their manufacturing enterprises a flock of several thousand head of hearty Merino sheep that they wished to have grazed in southern Idaho's "back country." As Ernie's father worked for the same company, it was no large matter to talk the "ramrod" into hiring young Ernesto to assume responsibility for a few hundred head of said flock.

Young Ernie was given instructions on where to escort his portion of the fold, a fine horse for the saddle, a pack mule laden with tent and supplies to last the summer, and the company of two expertly trained sheep dogs.

With what one must imagine as a tearful farewell, Ernie bade good bye to his father and mother, and gallantly made his way south into the vast, untamed reaches of the tri-state area, as one might well refer to that corner of the world which includes the boundaries of Idaho, Nevada, and Utah.

It was toward the middle of summer when young Ernie

discovered the ruins of a location he had heard his father and other shepherds speak of in words approaching awe. It was, Ernie earnestly assured me, The Gulch. Or, to utilize its full title, The Horse Thieves' Gulch.

El Dorado found! Or at least a treasure certain to quicken the pulse of even the most jaded historian.

Eagerly I asked for Ernesto's description of the famed outlaw hide-away, and with delighted ears I drank in his every word.

"There was a bunch of shacks and things, all of them starting to fall apart because of the heavy snows. It was all in an arroyo, up real high where they could see a posse coming for them."

"And the trading post?" I asked with unapologetic enthusiasm.

"Yes, that was there, too, but the roof was caved in. Too much snow is what I think."

My next question brought disappointment, not unexpected, but enough to momentarily quell my excitement. "Did men live there yet?"

But, alas, it was not to be. Quashing my desire for a "living relic" of another era, Ernie sadly shook his head in negation.

"Not for many years," he avouched.

My disappointment was keen but short-lived. I had, at long last, discovered proof, as glorious as it was indisputable, to be shouted to the pale blue heavens. Proof undeniable that the Outlaw Haven, now thusly named, did indeed exist.

I spoke with Ernesto Vasquez of this secret outlaw community at length, and will present my findings at the Public Library this coming Saturday at 7:00 P.M. Light refreshments will be served, and a small "donation" for my efforts to bring this discovery to light will be solicited at the door.

SESSION FIVE

Where was I . . . as if I don't remember feeling like a couple of locomotives were about to ram head-on right where I was standing. Oh, I trusted Lucy all right, but something was telling me to keep a wary eye on Della, at least until we got out of the gulch. That's why I had her pack the extra supplies while Lucy went to fetch Syd's palomino. I wasn't convinced Della wouldn't change her mind once she got outside, and make a beeline for Danson's.

Lucy was back within minutes, and she and I and Della hauled McCandles's limp form outside. I don't know if you've ever had to lug the body of an unconscious man anywhere before, but it ain't as easy as you might expect. For one thing, there isn't anything firm to grab onto when the brain isn't telling the body to keep a stiff spine. Plus, there are all those limbs poking out in five different directions—well, three in this case, as we had Ian's arms bound tight. Still, it's a fact few people are aware of that the human figure can bend in so many ways, and do so all at once, too.

On top of that, the palomino wasn't co-operating with our efforts to flop the outlaw's body across its back. It kept sidling one way or another, all the while tossing its head and snorting its displeasure. The horse even pitched a little the first time we came close to getting Ian into the saddle. The whole procedure probably would have been comical to watch on a city street, but I knew no one would be laughing if we were caught in the act, and with all the noise the palomino was making, it's a wonder we weren't.

I wasn't going to give up, though, and eventually we had Mc-Candles slumped over his saddle horn, lashed firmly in place.

"Now what?" Della asked. She was sweating heavily by then, wiping it off her forehead with the back of her bare arm. "We can't all four ride one horse."

"There's Carl's bay and Ben's sorrel out back," Lucy reminded her. "We can ride those." She looked at me. "Do you have a horse?"

"I've got Syd's gray stashed in some aspens down the trail."

We hurried around back with the supplies taken from the cabin, and I helped the women mount. I'll admit I caught an eyeful of Della, who was wearing a dress, yet seemed unfamiliar with any form of modesty. I was glad Lucy was wearing men's clothing. Not for propriety's sake, but because it made it easier for her to get on and off of a horse. Male attire would be warmer, too, and that was going to be critical in the days ahead.

Hammerhead was still in the aspens where I'd left him, and I swear he and the palomino were happy to see one another. They nickered back and forth a few times, so I was relieved when they stopped doing that and took to nuzzling each other like old friends, no doubt exchanging stories of the numerous hardships they'd been through since they'd last parted. I loosened the gray's reins and handed those and the palomino's lead rope to Lucy.

Della snorted. "What's the matter, bub? Don't you trust me?"

Palming Ian's nickel-plated Frontier Model Colt from the hand-tooled holster that I'd strapped around my waist before leaving the cabin, I handed it to Lucy. "If she makes so much as a peep, shoot her," I said.

"My, oh, my," Della said. "Ain't you the curly haired stud?" She looked at Lucy. "You ever take a shot at me, dearie, you'd better not miss, because I'll wring your skinny-a--ed neck like Sunday's chicken dinner."

"I've got one more thing I need to do," I told Lucy. "It won't take but a minute, so stay here. I'll be right back."

Lucy nodded, and I took off.

Keeping to the shadows as much as possible, I made my way to the main corral. Not a soul spotted me as I pulled the latch on the gate and swung it open. The horses inside took immediate notice of a stranger in their midst, but they didn't seem especially alarmed. I moved around to the rear of the herd, then suddenly jumped forward while waving my arms above my head, all the while making a sibilant rasp between my teeth that I hoped would sound like a disturbed timber rattler.

A few of the horses closest to me backed off, but that was about it. I swore softly at the lackluster response and began running back and forth, still swinging my arms wildly in the air. On the far side of the corral, several head began moving toward the gate. Others followed lazily. Soon the entire herd was drifting through the opening.

About half of the herd had cleared the gate when I heard a warning shout from Danson's post. I saw a man standing behind the building watering the weeds, one shoulder propped drunkenly against the log wall. I don't think he'd spotted me yet, but he'd sure taken notice of the escaping remuda.

Spend much time around livestock and you'll soon learn there isn't much that will bring a person to his or her feet faster than the exclamation: *The horses are out!*

It was the same here. In less than a minute, a dozen or more men, women, and children were spilling into the night, not only from Danson's post, but from some of the other cabins and shacks, as well. Everyone immediately began converging on the corral, circling wide around the herd to cut off its escape. Although my presence still hadn't been discovered, I figured it was only a matter of time, so when a little pinto mare showed up at my side, I didn't hesitate to grab a handful of mane and swing onto her back. The mare naturally spooked at my unfamiliar weight, and scooted deeper into the herd. Clamping my legs tight around her barrel, I screamed like a banshee, then followed that with a single round from the Evans, fired into the night sky.

A lot of things happened all at once then, not the least of which was my horse bolting like a terrified cat. Even expecting it, I was nearly unhorsed. The mare lined out for the gate with the rest of the herd surging forward around her. Even as I clawed for my seat, I was aware of the people who had been coming toward us now scattering like billiard balls.

With the gate wide open and unprotected, I drove my heels into the pinto's ribs. The horses were flowing like a river through the opening, a kaleidoscope of noise and color and motion. By the time anyone figured out what was going on, I was free of the corral and well on my way down the trail.

A few shots rang out behind me, but nothing came close. Coming to the aspens, I heeled the pinto away from the main herd, then swung a leg over the animal's neck and launched myself into the air.

You can get away with a stunt like that when you're seventeen. If I tried it today, I'd likely break every bone in my body, but that night in Horse Thieves' Gulch, I just tucked into myself like an armadillo and rolled. I came up on my feet not half a dozen yards away, and hurried into the trees without pause.

I was expecting the women to be ready to ride as soon as I got back, but instead I found everything falling apart as if someone had forgotten the glue. Della had lost her grip on the bay and it had bolted along with the stampeding remuda. She was still hanging onto the sorrel, but just barely. Meanwhile, Lucy had her hands full keeping the palomino and the gray under control. The palomino was especially jumpy with Ian McCandles strapped to its saddle. Ian was semi-conscious, moaning sickly and cursing between sprays of whiskey vomit. He was making a real mess of things, I'll tell you.

"What the h--- happened?" I shouted, earning myself a withering glance but no explanation.

"Grab something!" Lucy yelled in exasperation.

I took the gray's reins and pulled it around. With both hands free, Lucy soon had the palomino under control, but Della was still struggling with the sorrel. To make matters worse, I could hear the citizens of Horse Thieves' Gulch starting to rally.

I swung into the saddle and reined over to where Lucy was calming the palomino. Taking the lead rope from her hands, I told her to help Della. There was a lot of shouting coming from the upper end of the gulch, and I knew it wouldn't be long before they started in our direction. They'd come armed, too, and wouldn't be shy about emptying their guns at anything that moved.

"God d---it, get mounted," I commanded.

"What do you think we're trying to do?" Della fired back.

I peeked over my shoulder to where they had the sorrel pinned against the white bark of an aspen. The tree's golden crown shimmered in the pale starlight, loosening brief, rattling bursts of autumn leaves. Lucy was holding the sorrel's head as low as she could drag it while Della tried to jump astride the agitated gelding in her flouncing skirt. I could see they weren't going to accomplish anything that way, so I booted the Evans and rode over to take the sorrel's lead rope. Flashing me a grateful look, Lucy laced her fingers together like a flesh-and-bone stirrup. Della inserted a toe into the step and was quickly boosted astride. Then Lucy gave a jump and scrabbled up behind her. She'd barely gotten her seat when the first shot rang out from the gulch. The bullet tore off a chunk of bark

91

from a tree just a few feet away, and I shouted: "Let's go!"

I dug into the gray's ribs with my heels, the palomino practically clinging to my side as we burst out of the grove. Della and Lucy were close behind, but we'd lost precious time and the air around us was coming alive with the angry buzz of flying lead. There wasn't much we could do about it, though. Personally I kept my head low and prayed for poor aim.

None of us was shot on that crazy ride out of the gulch. Not even a scratch. We kept up a swift gallop for several miles, and only slowed down when I heard Della shouting for me to stop. Riding up close, she jutted her chin toward the palomino. "You're going to kill him if you keep this up."

I knew she wasn't talking about the horse, and I wasn't sure I cared about McCandles, but, when I spotted a little gully winding off to the south, I went ahead and reined into it. Not long after that, I pulled the gray to a stop.

Della jumped off her horse and ran over to where McCandles was draped over his saddle, having once again slipped into unconsciousness. She pushed his head up and started rubbing her hands over his face, lightly slapping his cheeks to bring him around. "If he dies, I'll cut your worthless throat," she told me.

That's the churchified version. Della hadn't left her salty tongue behind when we fled the gulch, and she wasn't sparing it any now.

"He'll be all right," I said, although I'll have to admit that in that skimpy light, McCandles's face didn't look very healthy. It kind of reminded me of a splash of dirty whitewash against rain-darkened lumber.

"Help me untie him," Della said.

"You just leave him where he is."

"He'll die if we don't get him off this horse."

"Joey, she's right," Lucy said. "Do you want him to die now, after all we've gone through just to get him this far?"

I wanted to tell them both that I didn't give a d--- one way or another, but I finally relented. I didn't want him to die like this. I wanted him to hang, and I wanted him to see that justice could prevail, no matter how tough the bandit. Walking over to where Della was whispering to McCandles, begging him to be tough and not give up, I loosened the rope binding his hands to the saddle horn, then freed his ankles. I didn't untie the rope around his wrists, though, and didn't intend to until I could turn him over to the law.

I'll confess that I was somewhat leery of McCandles, even in his trussed-up condition. I recalled how swiftly he'd reversed positions with me back at the cabin, and that with my rifle jammed into his belly and him three sheets to the wind on Danson's trade whiskey.

After hauling the gunman out of the saddle and tying his ankles, I led the palomino over to a patch of grass, where I loosened the cinch and removed the bridle so he could graze. Lucy did the same with the gray and the sorrel, and we soon had all three horses staked out and eating. I knew they needed water more than they did feed, and I was determined to find some as soon as it was light enough to see what we were doing. Lucy offered to fix some breakfast, but I told her not to bother, that we wouldn't be here long enough for that.

"I want to be well down the trail before the sun comes up," I told her.

"Then you'd better go get the horses right now," she said, nodding to the east, where the horizon was rimmed in a faint, pearled glow.

Where had the night gone? It seemed like only minutes ago that I'd crawled out of the trees to put the sneak on that lookout.

"Well, don't strike a fire," I said. "I don't want our smoke to be seen, in case we're being followed."

Della looked up from where she was tending to McCandles. "If you ain't sure they're following us, you're a bigger idiot than I originally took you for."

I handed Lucy the Colt. "Keep an eye on that one, too," I said, meaning Della. "I don't trust her."

Taking my Evans to hand, I crawled out of the gully, then up a razor-backed ridge until I could view our back trail. What I saw was discouraging. We hadn't come as far as I'd imagined. Even from here, I could still make out the northwest-running trail we'd followed in our flight from the gulch. The gully we'd turned into had a track like an arthritic snake, and for every hundred yards we covered on the ground, I doubt we'd gone more than fifty forward.

I crawled under a nearby piñon where I could keep an eye on the trail without being easily spotted by passers-by and made myself comfortable. Laying quiet like that, I began to think about what Della had said about us being pursued by McCandles's men. But would they? I'd noticed back at the Palace that no one had seemed overly fond of McCandles. Several of them had acted outright hostile. They seemed to believe he had tried to pull something shady by holing up in Coalville, rather than at Cedar Junction, where he'd said he'd be. If that was the way they felt, why would they bother coming after him now? Loyalty among thieves? Friendship? Brotherhood?

Not too d---ed likely, was my thinking, and for the first time since creeping into the gulch last night, I began to feel a modicum of hope that maybe I could pull this off. Maybe the McCandles gang wouldn't come after us, and all I had to do now was haul my human cargo back to civilization and turn the outlaw over to the authorities.

Caught up in that bubble of hope, I began to relax. Time passed and the light strengthened, pushing up into the underbelly of the night with a weight lifter's tenacity. It was still cold, though, and I set my rifle aside to cram my fingers under my armpits to keep them from going numb. My gloves were in my saddlebags, my heavy coat strapped behind the cantle with my bedroll. I was toying with the idea of going back to fetch them when I heard a distant shout. At first I thought it was coming from the trail, and I quickly scooped up my rifle. Then I heard it again, from behind me, and realized the commotion was coming from where I'd left Lucy with the horses.

Let me tell you, I came racing down off that ridge like a hawk after a crippled rabbit. I was jumping waist-high sage and dodging small junipers with an agility to make a fleeing deer envious. But I skidded to a stop quick enough when I came to the lip of the gully and saw Lucy on her back in the sand. Della stood above her with Ian's Colt in both hands. She was edging toward McCandles, but stopped when he called a warning. She looked at me. My rifle was pointed at her, but I was still holding it at waist level.

"Don't you move, bub!" Della yelled.

I looked at Lucy. She was sitting up, blood dribbling from her nose. "I was getting Ian something to eat, and Della jumped me," she explained.

"You stay right there," Della said, her eyes darting from me to Lucy, then back again. "Both of you."

"Shoot him, god d---it," McCandles urged. "Don't take any chances, kill the b------s and be done with it."

"I want to know one thing first," Della said to Ian, even as she kept her eyes fixed on me and Lucy. "Did you mean what you said the other night about us going to San Francisco?"

McCandles hesitated. I could tell that he didn't have any idea what she was talking about. Likely he'd given her some drunkard's promise of undying devotion, and she was desperate to believe it. It seemed an uncharacteristic response from a whore with her hardened reputation, but you've got to remember that I didn't know either one of them, then or now. I didn't know how long they'd been together, or what their circumstances might have been before I came along. I do know that McCandles's expression abruptly softened.

"Why, you can bet I meant every word of it," he said, grinning like a snake-oil salesman. "You and me, darlin'. We'll paint that town up one side and down the other."

It was an obvious lie, and it seemed to hover over that gully like a swarm of blowflies over a rotting carcass, but it brought an instant smile to Della's face. She turned to show it to Ian. I might have been able to get off a shot in that brief moment of distraction, except that I had yet to chamber a second round after firing the Evans back at the corral. And just like that—a thump of a heartbeat, a blink of an eye—the opportunity was lost.

"Hurry over here and cut me loose," McCandles said, shoving his bound wrists toward her.

Della's smile never wavered. She shifted the Colt to her left hand, and with her right she pulled a short-bladed dagger from a sheath tucked inside her high-topped shoe. I've seen men do that, carry a sticker in their footwear—a boot knife, they call it—but I'd never known a woman to do so. It was a lesson in femininity I've never forgotten. Another lesson I learned at the same time was to never underestimate a woman. In this case, Lucy Lytle.

Della had me covered with the Colt, and she probably should have just gone ahead and shot me as McCandles had wanted. I honestly don't know why she didn't. Maybe it was just a mistake on her part, and not all that different from the numerous missteps I'd recently made, but she paid dearly for it. While she was covering me with the revolver and talking to McCandles and like as not making plans in her mind for the good life on Nob Hill, Lucy had quietly gotten her feet under her. When

Della turned to sever the rope binding McCandles's wrists, Lucy launched herself across that narrow gully like a bottle rocket.

Della's startled grunt as Lucy's compact form slammed into her from behind could be heard all over that hillside. Knife and revolver went spinning, and she and Lucy collided with the steep bank behind McCandles, kicking and scratching.

I'll say this for McCandles—he wasn't one to let a stroke of luck slide by without making a grab for it. I don't think either woman had even hit the ground before he was scrambling across the sandy wash after the revolver.

What I did next was pure instinct, but I reckon it saved my bacon. Sure as Hades, I wasn't going to have time to lever a fresh round into the Evans' chamber. Instead, what I did was jump straight into the fray, landing feet first on top of Ian's Colt before he could grab it. He cursed and threw himself against my knees and I went down hard. I tried to kick the revolver across the gully, but McCandles caught it by the barrel, then flipped it around so that the muzzle was pointed at my belly. Before he could get the hammer thumbed back into the firing position, though, I swung the Evans back-handed, the walnut stock cracking sharply against his cheek. He tumbled backward, the Colt spurting from his fingers as if greased with hot lard.

McCandles was down, but he wasn't finished. Even as I crabbed across the sandy wash for the revolver, he cocked his legs up close to his body, then lashed out like a mule with an attitude. His heels thudded into my ribs and I went sprawling. Rolling onto his knees, McCandles lunged for the revolver, but I wasn't done, either, and threw myself in the same direction.

We reached the Colt together, and for a while it was an even match. My limbs were free and I was young and wiry. I should have been a shoo-in to win, but McCandles was a brawler, and he had the scarred knuckles to prove it. It was like wrestling with a scalded cougar to keep him away from that revolver. I had sand in my eyes that I'm pretty sure wasn't by accident, and McCandles kept trying to butt me in the face with the back of his head. At one point, attempting to get my forearm around his throat, the son-of-a-b---- bit me hard enough on the soft web below my thumb to leave a pair of crescent-shaped indentations that would last well into the following year.

The thing is, I'm stubborn, and I always have been. I doubt if I would have survived into my teenage years if I hadn't been. So, no matter what McCandles tried or how hard he bucked, I hung on until I finally managed to slap the revolver across the gully, well out of his reach. As soon as I did that, I jumped off and scooped it up.

Wheeling sharp, I rocked the hammer back to full cock, and just like that, McCandles gave up. The man was reckless and mean and ruthless in battle, but he wasn't dumb. Flopping back on his butt, he brushed the hair from his forehead, revealing a pair of eyes like shards of cold blue glass. Sweat ran down his face and he was breathing hard, the way boozers and smokers generally do after any kind of exertion, but he didn't say a word. I would have figured him to cuss me until the air turned thick with hatred, but he just sat there catching his breath. I was soon to believe he was already planning ahead to his next escape attempt.

Getting to my feet, I lurched over to where Lucy and Della were still rolling around on the ground, wild-eyed and disheveled, their faces streaked with dirt and tears. Not that either of them was crying, mind you. No, their tears were from having their faces rubbed in the sandy soil. In addition to the grime, the shoulder of Della's dress had been ripped halfway down to her elbow, and the top two buttons on Lucy's shirt were missing, the collar gaping enough to reveal the beginning swell of her breasts.

Yeah, I noticed. I was seventeen, remember?

"Quit it," I said sharply. When they ignored my command and kept on wallowing across the gully's floor, I planted a solid kick to Della's behind. She yelped and jerked away, and Lucy, on her knees and out of breath, let her go.

"Get up," I ordered.

Della threw McCandles a dismayed look, but the outlaw leader merely shrugged.

"What happened?" I demanded of Lucy.

"I already told you."

"Well . . . don't ever turn your back on them again."

She shot me a belittling glare. Slouched back against the far wall of the gully, McCandles chuckled. "Sage advice, little girl. You'd do well to heed it." Then he looked at me, and his shady grin vanished. "Kid, you are in so far over your head you can't begin to fathom it."

"I can fathom it," I replied, although at the time I didn't even know what the word meant. I just didn't want McCandles to think he was gaining the upper hand in any way.

"I'll make you a deal," McCandles went on. "You cut me loose right now, and I'll give you my word that I won't kill you. H---, it ain't in my best interest to shoot you, anyway. I'd be wasting a good bullet."

"What you're wasting is good air by jabbering on like a half-wit," I told him. "You ought to shut your mouth before I decide to gag you."

"No, hear me out now," he said. "I can tell you've got a good heart, and that it's only your brain that's lacking, so I'll not only let you live, I'll let you have these two women, to boot. In fact, I'll let you keep my gun. You ain't going to get a fairer deal than that anywhere."

I said: "I've already got the women, and I've already got your gun. It doesn't appear to me that you're in much of a position to bargain."

"That's because you ain't looking at the big picture yet. It ain't guns or women I'm offering you. It's your life."

He'd been trying to raise my hackles with his talk of making a deal. He knew I wouldn't consider it. But his words did finally get to me. "One more puff of hot air out of you, and I'll shove my rifle butt down your gullet and tie it there," I threatened.

McCandles grinned like a man satisfied with the results of his labors, although I noticed he didn't have anything saucy to respond with. That's all I was wanting, for him to just shut up.

Getting to her feet, Lucy said: "What are we going to do now?"

"I reckon we'd better keep riding," I said. "We need to put some miles between us and that main trail out of the gulch. It ain't but a far spit away, and too close for my peace of mind."

"I'll bring in the horses."

When she was gone, I picked up Della's knife. "Give me the sheath," I said.

She called me a number of foul words, but then yanked a plain leather scabbard from her boot and threw it at me. I slid blade and sheath inside my own boot, then turned to the saddle tack piled nearby. Noticing a chunk of bread with some gooseberry jam and a thick slice of cold roast beef—slow elk, remember?—sitting on a saddle where Lucy had been preparing it for Ian, my belly grumbled. I went over and helped myself.

"I could use a bite of that myself," Ian said.

"You had your chance," I reminded him.

"Some food might settle my stomach. I'd hate to puke all over my boots. It might upset the ladies' delicate nature."

"I ain't worried. We can keep you downwind if we have to." I tore off a bite of tough meat and commenced chewing.

"You b------," Della said, glowering at McCandles. "You told me you loved me. You said you and me'd go to California."

"Yeah, and we'd be on our way now if you'd shot the kid like I told you to."

"You said you'd give me to him if he turned you loose!" Della shouted.

I think if McCandles had a gun at that moment he would have shot her. Then his mood seemed to do a complete flip, and he flashed her a toothy grin. "Well, sure, but only if you wanted to go."

Della hesitated. I could tell she was running McCandles's reply over in her mind, trying to make sense of it, but I already had him pegged. He would string her along to his own advantage for as long as it took, but, when he was sure he had no further use for her, he'd dump her like an unwanted apple core.

My distaste for the gunman was growing steadily.

Lucy returned with the horses and began saddling them. She looked angry and subdued and in no mood for me to offer her a helping hand, so I stayed out of her way and finished my breakfast. When the horses were ready, I handed her the Colt. "This time . . . ," was all I got out before she shut me off.

"This time, I'll blow her blankety-blank head off," she said, and I could tell that Della believed her. You've likely already guessed it wasn't *blankety-blank* that she called the older woman, either.

Leaning the Evans against the side of the bank, I walked over to where McCandles was sitting. He laughed at the wary expression on my face, and, when I started to reach for him, he jerked his still-bound feet toward me and shouted: *"Boo!"*

I ain't proud to admit that I flinched and jumped back, but I said I'd tell you the truth about what happened out there, and I won't whitewash anything. Not even the parts that reflect poorly on me.

From behind me, Lucy said: "If you can't handle him now,

Joey, you might as well turn him loose and ride out of here."

"That's an option I'd heartily recommend," McCandles said. "Give it up while you're still alive, kid. You've proved your point."

Taking a deep breath, I reached for McCandles's feet, intending to loosen them so he could mount. Once again, he feigned a double-heeled kick, but this time I was ready for him. Snatching the rope connecting his ankles, I hauled him over to the palomino like a sack of grain.

I half expected the outlaw to try something underhanded while I put him in the saddle, but he could tell I was on the prod, and turned as docile as an old cart pony.

Della had ridden behind Lucy in our race away from the gulch, but I didn't want that combination on top of the sorrel again. I put Della up behind McCandles, then stretched her arms around the outlaw's waist to tie her wrists to the saddle horn where McCandles was already hitched.

"See, darlin', we're as cozy up here as we'd be in a feather bed in San Francisco," McCandles said, but Della didn't respond.

It was quick work to get everyone mounted and lined out to the south. I took the forward position, keeping the palomino with its dangerous cargo just a few steps behind me on the end of its lead rope. Lucy brought up the rear on the sorrel, her mood unimproved.

SESSION SIX

You know, even today, I don't know the name of the mountain range where I found Lucy and took Ian McCandles into custody. I don't know if it was in Idaho or Nevada or Utah, but it was in that general area. I'm not saying I was lost, because I wasn't. Not in that hopeless, don't-know-which-way-to-turn kind of way, but it was an unknown country to me, and I was leading mostly on instinct.

We kept moving south all that first day. Not pushing it, mind you, for the horses were already half worn-out after the long ride from Coalville, but we weren't taking time to admire the scenery, either.

It's a wonder my head didn't come unscrewed from the way I kept swiveling it around to keep an eye on my prisoner—I wasn't sure yet where Della fell in the equation. I kept expecting more trouble from McCandles, but he behaved himself the whole day long.

Oh, I didn't trust that bird, not one little bit, but I wasn't going to look a gift horse in the mouth, either. We were making pretty good time for such a torturous country, and I savored the uneventfulness of the passing hours as I would a good meal or a full night's sleep.

Just keep moving, I repeated to myself about a dozen times that day.

Toward dusk we came to a shallow rill and stopped to water our horses. Because the grass was still green on both sides of the brook, I decided to camp there for the night.

Getting Ian and Della off the palomino wasn't nearly as cumbersome as it had been to get them on. I untied Della first and hauled her from the saddle's rear skirt. She just about toppled to the ground when I let go of her, she was so stove-up from riding all day. With McCandles, I uncinched the saddle and pulled it off, rider and all. I tried to catch him to break the fall, but he ended up smacking the ground hard enough to jar loose a couple of colorful epithets. I walked away leaving him there on his side, straddling his saddle.

I won't mention that I handed my guns to Lucy every time I got within striking distance of McCandles. You're going to have to take my word for that. I will say this. When it came to handling risky characters, I was learning.

There were stunted junipers in every direction, and I sent Della out with Lucy to collect a couple of armfuls of dead stuff. I didn't intend to keep a fire burning all night because I wasn't totally convinced we weren't being followed, but I'd seen Della pack some coffee in our gear back at her cabin, and I was hankering for a cup. My eyeballs were starting to feel like clay marbles inside their sockets, dry and itching and needing to be shut for more than just a few minutes at a time. I was hoping some coffee might lessen the discomfort.

We made a small fire with the driest wood in the stack so that we wouldn't produce too much smoke, and Lucy whipped up a kettle of coffee, patted out fresh ash cakes, and warmed up some of Della's slow elk to take the chill off. I hadn't been able to see my breath all day, but with the sun going down it was coming back in little blue-gray puffs.

It was still light in the west when we finished eating, the clouds twisting around themselves like gold and ruby threads, but, as darkness came on, I ordered the women to let the fire die.

Eyeballing me from across the coals, a tiny smile lifted the corners of McCandles's mouth. "Well, kid, the moment of truth has arrived. I gotta hit the bushes." He held his hands up in front of him. "And I can't do it wrapped up like a ham for the smokehouse."

Now, that was a matter I hadn't considered. Me and Lucy and even Della—we'd loosened her wrists to gather wood and hadn't retied her—could just wander off and do our business whenever the need arose, but there wasn't any way in h--- I was going to allow McCandles that kind of freedom.

I glanced at Lucy, who snorted contemptuously and walked away. I turned to Della. She shot me a dark look and a gesture with her middle finger that I figure we'd all recognize. Standing grudgingly, I hoisted the Evans. "Della can untie your feet so you can walk," I told him, "but you're going to have to do the rest of it with your hands tied."

McCandles's eyes narrowed. "I can't take care of myself with my hands like this. They're already half numb from lack of circulation."

"That ain't my problem," I replied, making a couple of upward motions with the Evans' muzzle to start him to his feet. "I told you this morning I could stake you downwind if you messed yourself, and I meant it. Now let's get this taken care of while it's still light enough for you to see what you're grabbing. I'd hate like h--- for you to pick some poison oak by mistake."

McCandles glared but stood. I reckon he really did have to go.

All I'm going to say on this subject from here on is that Ian McCandles proved to be more flexible than I would have given him credit for, and, although he complained about it every time he had to go into the bushes, he always managed to take care of his needs in a manner that kept his long-handles clean.

I tied Della up that night and double checked Ian's bindings, then hitched them both to junipers not far away. I gave each of them a blanket, and told McCandles: "I wouldn't wiggle around too much, thinking you're going to get loose. If you pull that blanket off during the night, you'll be halfway to an icicle by sunup."

For the first time since leaving the gulch, McCandles's poise broke, if only for a minute. "I'm gonna kill you slow, kid," he promised. "I'm gonna make you suffer like you ain't never suffered before."

"If you don't hang first," I reminded him, pleased as punch that I'd finally cracked his hard veneer.

I was fair exhausted, and I don't mind admitting it. Lucy bedded down next to the fire, even though it had died and was covered in ash. Taking my bedroll, I walked out into the brush. I wanted to be able to hear anyone approaching and not mistake it for someone tossing under their blanket. Turns out, as dead to the world as I slept that night, I might as well have crawled into a gopher hole and pulled the dirt in on top of me.

The sky was already light and I could hear Lucy puttering around in camp when I finally pried open my eyes the next morning. Lordy, I think I could have snoozed the day away, I was so tired. I shrugged into my heavy coat, then pulled on my shoes. My fingers tingled from the cold as I tightened the laces. Walking back to camp, I found Lucy kindling a fresh blaze on top of last night's coals. I almost told her to put it out because I wanted to leave first thing, but I could see she was feeling frosty—in more ways than one.

"We're going to keep a fire burning tomorrow night," she told me. "I don't intend to freeze my a-- off again just 'cause you're scared."

Even though her nose looked about as red as a Christmas ornament, I had my concerns about lighting a beacon for others to see. "Do you figure Della is right about McCandles's boys following us?" I asked, hunkering down opposite her and thrusting my hands toward the flames.

Lucy poked at the crackling wood as if stalling for time. Not a good sign, I decided. "Probably," she said after a long pause.

"Why?"

She kept prodding at the fire, as if weighing her response. Finally she sighed and looked up. "I don't know the whole story, but from what I gathered on the ride out here, McCandles has got a bunch of gold stashed away somewhere."

"Gold? Where'd he get gold?"

"Where do most highwaymen get gold?"

"You mean he robbed someone?"

"D---it, ask him. I ain't a member of his gang."

"No, but I figure you'll tell me the truth, which is more than I'd count on from those two." I made a motion toward where Ian and Della were still tied up, shivering under their blankets.

Tossing her stick into the flames, Lucy said: "All I know is what I pieced together from listening to him and his men at the Palace, then on the way out here. They robbed a stagecoach up the road toward Boise, but had to split up when the law got too close. McCandles and a guy called Long Pete took the strongbox with them on the back of Pete's horse, on account of him being more or less as runty as you are. They were all supposed to meet at Cedar Junction to split up the money, then take off again in different directions, only McCandles didn't show up at the junction. He came to Coalville instead. Trouble was, Long Pete wasn't with him any more.

"The boys figured McCandles was trying to skip out with the gold, but McCandles told them Cedar Junction had been a poor choice for a rendezvous, being on the main road between Kelton and Boise. He said if he'd really intended to run, he would have been halfway across Utah by the time the rest of them got to Coalville. Some of his men believed him, others didn't. It's been enough so far to keep McCandles alive, but they still don't have the loot he ditched."

"Where's it at?"

"He ain't been real specific as far as I can tell, but he mentioned a place called City of Rocks."

"City of Rocks?"

"You know where that is?"

"I've heard of it, but I've never been there."

Lucy's interest was definitely piqued by my reply. "Do you think you could find it?"

From what I'd heard, City of Rocks was a rough stretch of country in the central part of southern Idaho. It's pretty high up, with a lot of cedars and piñon pines and such. There was supposed to be fair grass for grazing and good water the year 'round, but mostly it's a hellacious maze of oddly shaped pinnacles jutting into the clouds like a New York City skyline.

I make that comparison to New York from postcards I've seen of the place. I've never personally been there.

"Yeah, I could probably find it," I told her. "They say it's a pretty big place, though. A strongbox full of gold wouldn't be easy to find without a map."

Lucy jerked her head toward McCandles. "What do we need a map for? We've got him."

"You mean go get it now?"

"Why not?"

The fact that I had my hands full with McCandles was the first why not to pop into my mind. Tight on the heels of that was Lucy and Della's safety, which, to my way of thinking, I had taken responsibility for. Add to that the likelihood that McCandles's gang would soon be hot on our trail and you had three very good reasons to keep riding for Coalville just as fast as our ponies could carry us.

But even as all of that went careening through my brain like a runaway buggy, I had to admit, it would be icing on the cake if I could bring in not only Ian McCandles, but the loot he and his gang had stolen off that Boise coach. It might go a long way toward sealing McCandles's fate when he got in front of a judge and jury, too, I reasoned.

Pushing abruptly to my feet, I said: "I need to think about it."

"What's there to think about?"

"A lot of things," I replied, recalling, on top of everything else, our limited supply of food, blankets, and horses. I tried to explain my reasoning to Lucy, but she just started frowning almost before I got started.

"I never took you for a coward," she finally cut in.

Now, I might have only been seventeen, but even I knew what she was trying to do with a statement like that.

"That won't work," I said. "Not after my hauling you out of the middle of an outlaw's camp."

She eyed me thoughtfully for a moment, then casually brushed her jacket back to reveal the man's flannel shirt she was wearing underneath. She did it like she wasn't even thinking about it, but she knew what she was doing, and so did I. Staring into the fire, she fiddled with the button nearest her collar, not counting the two she'd lost in her scrape with Della yesterday. She'd loosen it, then fasten it again, then loosen it once more, and I'll confess that my eyes never strayed far from the pale shadow of her cleavage, flashing in and out of my view. It didn't change my mind, though.

"What if they're waiting for us on the way back to Coalville?" she asked. "We could ride straight into them going that way."

"There's a hundred ways back to Coalville from here."

"What if they split up? We wouldn't have any idea where they were until it was too late."

She left the top button undone and began fingering the next

one down. My throat was growing thick and my eyes must have felt like hot coals on her pale flesh. When the next button came undone, I swallowed audibly and turned away. I could see Mc-Candles watching us from the juniper's shadow, intrigued by the show Lucy was putting on and no doubt wondering what it was all about.

After a long pause, she stood and rebuttoned her shirt, then pulled her jacket closed. The moment was over and I'd won, but just barely.

"Get some breakfast started," I said. "I'll bring in the prisoners."

I freed Della and told her to bring in an armload of wood when she came back from the bushes. Then I went over to where McCandles lay like a lump of hardened clay.

"You and that gal have got something planned?" he observed.

"Nothing that's any of your concern," I replied, reaching for the rope knotted around his ankles.

That's when he made his move. Like lightning, he struck out at my face with his heels, filling my eyes with the soles of his boots. I had been distracted by Lucy. Not so much her unsubtle efforts at seduction, but by the prospects of finding the gold and returning it to its rightful owners. Yet even distracted, something must have kicked in inside my feebled brain, because this time I managed to dodge the worst of the outlaw's double-barreled kick. Only one of his heels caught me, and that just in the shoulder. Although it spun me back and around, I didn't fall, and, when McCandles lunged for my knees, I parried him off with a solid blow to the back of his neck.

McCandles hit the ground with a loud grunt, then brought his bound wrists up to rub the back of his head. That was when something happened that I'd never experienced before. You've heard people claim to see red when they're angry? Well, that's just about what it's like. In my case, a pinkish mist clouded my vision, and there was a roaring in my ears like a coal-powered generator running past the red line. I grabbed the narrow stretch of rope between McCandles's ankles and roughly hauled him around. He swore and sputtered as I dragged him to the fire, but I didn't slow down, and I sure as Hades didn't take the easiest path I could find. I hauled him through sage and over cactus buds like so much meat, then dropped his legs so that his toes spiked the hot coals.

He wasn't aware of it at first, but he started cursing anew when he felt the heat searing through the leather of his boots. He howled and jerked his legs up to get his feet out of the fire. Rolling over on his side, he spat at me, and that's when I did something I've never told anyone before. But I'm going to tell you, and, if you think the less of me for it, then so be it.

I kicked him. McCandles, I mean. I hauled back and kicked that s.o.b. in the ribs just as hard as I could, and that was plenty, as mad as I was.

I thought for a minute I'd killed him, the way he gasped and gagged and flopped around like a fish on a riverbank. He made a bunch of little mewing sounds like he couldn't breathe, and I guess he couldn't. Not right away. When he finally slowed down and started drawing in great, ragged gulps of air, I looked up to see Lucy staring at me from across the fire, smiling like a fox with a bunch of chicken feathers caught in its whiskers.

"You're starting to learn, Joey," she said.

I knew she meant it nicely, but I was in no mood for puffery. "I told you to get breakfast started," I said. "Get your a-- moving, because we're heading for City of Rocks just as soon as we're finished eating."

CITY OF ROCKS
NATIONAL PRESERVE
COMPILATION OF IDAHO AND
NATIONAL PARKS SERVICE
BROCHURES
2010

City of Rocks is located within the Albion Mountain Range in south-central Idaho, on the northern edge of the Great Basin. These unique granite formations, some towering as high as six hundred feet, provide breathtaking scenery and unparalleled photographic opportunities.

A rock-climber's dream, they . . . became a landmark in 1843 for California-bound emigrants. The fourteen thousand four hundred and seven acre reserve boasts Idaho's tallest piñon pines, at more than fifty-five feet in height. These piñon forests are the largest in the state. . . .

Embracing a sagebrush steppe valley, spectacular granite rock formations, piñon/juniper tree stands, and alpine-like meadows, the reserve presents an inspirational landscape. Recreational activities include hiking, wildlife viewing, rock climbing, backpacking, Nordic skiing, photography, and horseback riding. The City of Rocks Visitor Center is located in Almo.

Established by Congress in 1988 as a National Reserve . . . lands containing grand scenery, rich cultural history, and places of . . . solitude and silence.

SESSION SEVEN

I wasn't an experienced traveler in those days, but I'd kept track of my surroundings while following the McCandles gang west from Coalville, and I had a pretty fair idea where we were on the morning that I decided to retrieve the stolen gold. Getting everyone mounted—Lucy on the sorrel, McCandles hitched tight to his saddle atop Syd's palomino with Della behind him, her wrists bound around his belly, and me on Hammerhead—we headed due east.

City of Rocks lay to the northeast, but so did the mountain range where McCandles and his men had elected to hole up, and I wanted to avoid that country as much as possible. We kept the southern foothills of the higher range on our left, and made good progress. No one talked much, which I considered a blessing. We stopped for a while early in the afternoon to water our horses and refill our single canteen at a small stream, then pushed on. I saw nary a soul all day save for birds and sunning lizards and some antelope off in the distance—too far to waste a shot on, too wary to stalk. Antelope is good eating, but you've got to know how to skin them to keep the goat stink off.

We came to a stand of cottonwoods in the bottom of a small depression about an hour before dark, and I made the decision to camp for the night. There was water and wood and good grass for the horses, and our fire would be sheltered from both the wind and prying eyes by a low bluff just above the trees.

I tied off the gray, then walked over to the palomino. "Mc-

113

Candles," I said, "I am plum weary of your trouble-making ways, so if you've got a notion to give me any more of it tonight, I'd suggest you get it out of your head right now."

McCandles looked at me like I was a pile of horse apples dumped in the middle of the kitchen floor. "Kid, I don't intend to ride back with you to that piece of c--- town you call home. Is that answer enough?"

I reckoned it was, but I still needed to get him off his horse. Not for his sake, mind you, but for the palomino's. I loosened Della's wrists and she slid off and hobbled away. With Mc-Candles, I did as before, just freed the cinch and gave him a push. He started cussing a blue streak as soon as he saw what I intended to do, and kept it up all the way to the ground before he finally shut up to concentrate on catching his breath.

I'd bound McCandles's wrists to the saddle horn a whole lot tighter than Della's, and I could see that his fingers were puffed up like sausages. Just about the same color, too. I'd lashed his knees to the cinch ring on either side of the saddle, although not as tight. Loosening those, I hauled him to his feet. He came up fast, swinging the saddle like a club, but it was too cumbersome to do much damage. Especially now that I had him figured out. I grabbed the fender as the saddle came close and gave it a hard yank, sending McCandles flying into some nearby scrub. He struggled for a few minutes to free himself, then just flopped back with the saddle in his lap, chest heaving.

"That was foolish," I told him. But when I bent down to free him from the brush, I'll be d---ed if he didn't land a kick to my groin. I stumbled back with a drawn-out groan, and McCandles lunged to his feet as easy as jumping up from the breakfast table. I saw the saddle arching above his head just before it slammed down on top of me. Something caught me hard, either the cantle or one of the wooden stirrups, and I hit the ground face first. When I rolled over, McCandles was standing over me with the saddle cocked above his shoulder to strike me a second time. Then a gunshot exploded from somewhere off to my left and McCandles froze. When he did, I drove my heel into his knee as hard as I could, and he dropped as if pole-axed, shrieking all the way to the ground.

I got to my feet and limped over to where Lucy stood beside a pile of unlit kindling. I reached for the revolver but she took a swift step back and swung the muzzle to cover my chest.

"No," she said.

"What?"

"Just . . . let me think."

"Give me the gun, d---it."

"Back up, Joey! I mean it!"

"The h--- I will," I said. But when I took a step forward, she thumbed the hammer back to full cock.

I stopped in my tracks, staring down the dark bore of McCandles's Frontier Model Colt. "Easy," I said gently, as if talking to a frightened horse.

"Shut up, Joey. Please, just . . . shut up."

"Shoot him," Della urged in her gravelly voice.

"You shut up, too," Lucy said.

"You know he ain't got what it's gonna take to pull this off," Della said. "Ian's gonna get the upper hand sooner or later. Then where're you and me gonna be?"

I glanced at the Evans, leaning against a tree at Lucy's side. It might as well have been back in Coalville for all the good it was going to do me there.

Although McCandles was still on the ground, he'd stopped his howling and moaning to watch. Now, in a voice made harsh with pain, he said: "Della's right, girl. If you don't pop a cap on your little friend there, one of my boys soon will. They can't be more than a few hours behind, if that far. H---, like as not they're close enough now to've heard that shot." His eyes narrowed calculatingly. "Give me the gun, 'cause if you don't, and I'm still tied up like a d---ed hog when the boys get here, I'm gonna make sure it goes almighty hard on you. That's a promise."

Lucy looked at me. "He's right, Joey. You're a good kid, but you ain't no match for the McCandles gang."

"I'm taking him in, Lucy, no matter what you think or what he says."

"He'll kill you, or one of his men will. Life doesn't mean anything to them."

"It means something to me. They killed Ruby Davidson. Did you know that?"

Lucy sucked in a deep breath, and I could tell she hadn't known.

"They shot Syd Hackett, and I reckon he's dead now, too, along with a couple of the Hop Along's night crew. Then they burned the Palace."

Lucy was shaking her head frantically. "What do I care?" she cried.

"Lucy ain't worried about yesterday, boy," McCandles said. "Smart girl like that's already thinking about tomorrow. Ain't that right, darlin'?"

"You shut up, too." Lucy swung the Colt back on McCandles. "What you did to me . . . like a god d---ed dog. . . ." She tried to say more, but the words choked off.

"I wasn't hard on you," McCandles said. "It was me that kept the rest of the boys off of you, remember? I could've let 'em have at you, if I'd wanted."

"You'd keep them off only until you got tired of her," Della said. "Just like you did me, you rotten son-of-a-b----." She looked at Lucy. "They won't ever let us go, honey. They'd be afraid we'd tell the law where they're holed up."

There was a low sound from McCandles's throat, like a dog's

chesty rumble right before it attacks. "You would, too, you worthless b----." He tried to get to his feet, but couldn't because of the saddle tied to his wrists and the busted knee I'd given him. "Don't listen to her, Lucy," he said. "All that matters is that you give me that gun right now. Do that, and I swear I won't hurt you, but if you don't, by G--, I'll carve my initials in your face."

He meant to cow her, you see, but his threat had the opposite effect. Lucy snapped off a shot that kicked up dust so close to McCandles's hip I thought surely he'd been hit.

"Shut up!" she screamed. "All of you, shut up!"

Nobody said a word, and I do believe she would have shot the first one of us who did. She moved back, as if to step clear of the confusion. Her face was dirty, tears channeling through the grime, and her nose was red and running snot from the cold. Right at that moment she didn't look the least bit intimidating, but she sure as Hades had us riveted in place. Of course, McCandles's revolver had a lot to do with that.

"Joey," she finally said.

"What?"

She hesitated so long I began to wonder if she'd forgotten what she was going to say. Then she walked over and handed me the Colt. I breathed a sigh of relief. McCandles glared daggers, and Della looked stunned.

"If you ever let him get the drop on you again," Lucy told me, "I promise you I'll give him the pistol and let him do whatever he wants with it."

"Take a look at him," I said. "If you ever give him anything to use as a weapon, he'll kill you with it as surely as he would me."

"I don't care," she said. "I'll do it. I swear I will." Then she walked off to gather more firewood. After a stormy look in my direction, Della followed her.

Remembering what Della had told Lucy about McCandles

never letting her go, I wondered again whose side she was on. I suppose Della herself couldn't have answered that with any certainty.

McCandles began exploring his injured knee as best he could with his swollen fingers. "I believe you did some serious damage here, kid," he said.

"I'll do worse the next time."

He chuckled without looking up. "I expect you'll want to, but I won't fail next time."

He hadn't totally failed this time, although I didn't tell him that. I was feeling real gimpy between the legs, and I was glad we'd stopped for the night. I'm not sure I could have forked a saddle right then.

It was a real sullen evening. Della didn't say anything, just stared into the flames as if in a trance, and Lucy barely spoke. She kept the fire burning all night, and I didn't say anything against it. It was cold enough that I consented to let Della and McCandles sleep close to the fire, although I did retie Della's wrists, just in case. I left McCandles's ankles unfettered. If you'd seen the size of his swollen knee stretching the rough fabric of his trousers, you'd understand why. He hadn't been lying when he said I'd done him some serious hurt. I ain't saying I felt sorry for him, but it wasn't my intention to inflict torture on the man, either.

I was up before dawn the next morning and had the outfit mounted and on the trail before sunup. We'd made steady progress toward the morning side all day yesterday, so I was turning us north today. According to my mental calculations, City of Rocks was about a day and a half to two days north by a hair east of where we were now, and I wanted to get us in there and out again as quickly as possible.

Nobody spoke as the morning wore on. McCandles rode hunched to one side to allow his injured leg to dangle freely. I hadn't taken a look at it, but I could see it was still horribly enlarged.

The land we traveled through that day was a lot rougher than what we'd traversed the day before, and our pace was slowed accordingly. It was noon before it warmed up enough for me to shuck my heavy coat.

Yeah, I kept the coat for myself. I guess I should have done the gentlemanly thing and offered it to Lucy or Della, but I didn't. I tell myself now that I was feeling kind of trance-like by then, and wasn't really thinking clearly, or that Lucy had a jacket and they both had blankets they could drape over their shoulders. But the fact is, it wasn't very gallant, and it wasn't very heroic. Maybe now you can see why I don't like being called a hero.

We stopped at noon to rest the horses like we always did, picketing them on good grass below some aspens that would provide us with shade and a place to lean our backs. While the horses stretched and rolled and Lucy kept an eye on Ian and Della—without the revolver; I'd determined to keep that with me after what had happened last night—I climbed to the top of a nearby ridge to view our back trail. I wasn't really expecting to see anything—heck, I'd been doing this a couple of times a day ever since we'd fled the gulch—so you can imagine my surprise when I spotted a cloud of dust maybe eight or ten miles back.

What followed my initial astonishment was a sinking in my gut, like I'd just swallowed a horseshoe. After watching the dust for fifteen or twenty minutes, there was no doubt in my mind that there were horsemen under it, and that they were following our trail. The deliberateness of their progress belied any chance of it being some kind of wild game, like a herd of antelope or mustangs.

My throat went dry and my spirits hit the ground without

even a hint of a bounce. My first instinct was to race back down the ridge and get everybody mounted so that we could make a run for Coalville, the gang's stolen loot be d---ed. Fortunately I was able to rein in my panic before it overwhelmed my thinking. Taking off in a dither now would only wear out our horses, already taxed and overburdened. I had to *think* if I wanted to outfox a pack of foxes.

I made my way back to where the others were lounging in the shade. Only Lucy looked up as I approached. I tipped my head toward the horses, and she followed me over.

"Is it them?" she asked, sensing that the news was bad.

"Probably, but they're still a long way off."

"They can't be that far away if you saw them."

"All I saw was their dust. Look, we've got to come up with some kind of a plan, because we sure as h--- can't outrun them."

A look of terror spread across her face. I wondered if she was regretting her decision to hand over the revolver last night, maybe thinking that, if she'd given it to McCandles instead, she'd be in a better position now. It was something to keep in mind, I decided, and wondered then if I'd been putting too much trust in her.

"What do we do?" she asked.

"Go get the horses. If we can stay in front of them until nightfall, we can switch directions in the dark and maybe lose them that way."

Lucy hurried off to bring in our mounts. I went back to get McCandles and Della on their feet. I wasn't going to tell them about McCandles's men closing in on us, but something must have given it away. Hobbling over with his saddle dragging the ground, Ian smiled and winked. Oh, how I wanted to punch the smugness off his face. But I didn't. We were running short on time as it was.

There is a pattern to most mountain ranges, and this one was no different. Ridges and cañons coming down off the highest summits, more ridges and cañons, not quite as deep, coming off of those, then smaller and more shallow ridges and cañons, continuing on that way until flat ground is reached or another clump of mountains rears its snow-capped peaks. I've never flown, but I suspect that if you looked down from one of those aeroplanes that pass over every few days, you could see it real good from up there. Kind of like what an eagle sees everyday, but from behind a window.

Anyway, I mentioned the ridges and cañons because I wanted you to know what kind of country we were riding through. Stick to the cañons and you could make good time; cross the ridges and it goes a lot slower. We'd been staying to the ridges mostly because I wanted to make tracking us as difficult as possible, but when we rode out of those aspens it was straight downcañon, and no one had to ask why.

These cañons ain't like what you might imagine if you live out on the plains or in the Southern swamps or amidst the cornfields of the Midwest. A lot of folks picture them as all straight up and down, but the reality is that most of the cañons in this part of the country aren't sheer-sided at all. They're steep-walled, for a fact, covered with grass and brush and crumbling rocks, but if a man wanted to ride out of one, he could do it. It would be a chore, and he might have to dismount to lead his horse part of the way, but it could be done.

So, getting back to what happened. We rode down that cañon as fast as the terrain would allow. I knew that if we continued to follow the cañons we'd eventually come out well to the east of where I wanted to be, but I figured it was more important that we keep making good time. The only real trouble I saw was that our course would eventually put us out in open country on horses already jaded from hard riding. If we didn't throw off pursuit before then, we were going to be in real trouble.

121

Thinking about our flagging mounts got me to considering our options. One, which I dismissed after some thought, was to ride back into the higher peaks as soon as it got dark. It might have worked for a while, because they sure as Hades wouldn't be expecting it, but it would also put us right back at the mouth of the lion's den, so to speak, and that was something I wanted to avoid.

Another idea I toyed with was for us to make a run for Boise City. I'd never been to Boise, but I'd heard it was a thriving little town, with a population large enough to stand up to the likes of Ian McCandles and his gang. I didn't dwell too much on the fact that Coalville could have done the same thing, had its leading citizens not elected to hide in a darkened café while a bunch of thugs took over the town.

Did I mention I'm still bitter about that?

Anyway, Boise is on the Snake River, and I knew the Snake wouldn't be hard to find. Once we hit the river, we could just follow that on up to civilization, or wherever it was that the law might be hanging out in those parts.

The problem I had with making a run for Boise reflects poorly upon my own judgment in those tender years of my life, but the fact was, I didn't want Ian McCandles to hang for whatever crimes he'd committed up that way. I wanted him to hang for what he and his ruffians had done in Coalville—killing Syd Hackett and Ruby Davidson and those two Hop Along miners, ransacking the town, stealing horses out of Herb Smith's livery, setting fire to the Palace. I wanted justice.

No, d---it, I wanted *revenge*. Not just for what they'd done to Coalville, but for what they'd taken away from me personally, and I don't mean material things. I'm talking about the emotional ties I'd had to the town and its people. I'd been little more than a guttersnipe there for most of my life, but, by God, it had been my gutter.

No, sir! I knew if I kept pushing for home I might eventually fail, but I was determined to hang onto my original goal of seeing Ian McCandles returned to Coalville to stand trial for his crimes there. Either that or die trying.

Lost in anger, I was caught completely off guard when the palomino grunted sharply and bolted. From the corner of my eye, I saw McCandles gouge the palomino's ribs with the heel of his good leg.

The lead rope sizzled through my fingers like a hot branding iron. I cursed and let go, then kicked my horse after McCandles's fleeing mount. Lucy came pounding after me on the sorrel.

It was a futile effort on McCandles's part. He had to know that. With his wrists still lashed to the saddle and Della bouncing wildly behind him, there was no possible way he was going to escape. In fact, watching Della's screaming gyrations—she was showing ten or twelve inches of empty space between her ample rump and the saddle's skirting with every forward lunge—it's a wonder she didn't spill off altogether, dragging McCandles with her.

That would have been a bloody mess, with both of them still bound to the saddle, but, tough little whore that she was, she hung on and McCandles managed to turn the palomino into a side cañon.

The route was all uphill now, but McCandles kept pounding at the horse's ribs, urging it into an energy-draining run that would soon leave the animal winded, if not outright crippled. But, of course, he didn't care about the horse. It was his own neck he was thinking of.

Then something happened that caught all of us flat-footed. A body of horsemen appeared suddenly in the middle of the trail, and the palomino skidded to such a dirt-showering halt that Della was thrown off the side. It was OK, though. She kept her feet, and, as soon as the palomino came to a full stop, she quickly scrambled back up behind McCandles.

I'll bet you're thinking it was some of the McCandles's gang who had outflanked us, but it wasn't. It was Indians, probably twenty or more of them spread out across the cañon floor, arrows nocked, rifles cocked.

Bringing Hammerhead to a stop, I eased up alongside the palomino and reached carefully for the lead rope. Speaking quietly, McCandles said: "Let me handle this, kid."

"You just keep your mouth shut."

"Those are Bannocks, boy, and they ain't to be trifled with."

Now, there were Bannocks, Utes, Paiutes, Shoshones, and other tribes scattered all over that country, and, while we weren't technically at war at the time with any of them, I'd never known an Indian I'd want to trifle with. There were hard feelings on both sides of the race issue, back then and today, and a party of poorly armed whites with two good horses, a ewe-necked gray, and a couple of handsome women was no doubt a nice surprise for them.

I could see their eyes nervously working the ridge tops, looking for a trap, but it wouldn't take them long to realize that what they saw was all they were going to get. Assuming they wanted us. That was the question. They had us outnumbered by a wide margin, but they weren't making any hostile gestures yet.

For several minutes we had us a staring contest, me and Ian sitting our horses danged near stirrup-to-stirrup, while Lucy crowded her sorrel close behind the two of us as if trying to blend into the scenery. Maybe she was thinking they wouldn't notice that she was a woman since she was wearing men's clothing, but I suspect Lucy could have worn a suit of armor and we would have all recognized her for a female. She was that kind of a gal.

There was an elderly warrior toward the center of the line,

but, after a couple of minutes of uneasy silence, it was a younger Indian who spoke. Everybody watched as he pulled his buckskin out of the queue and rode over beside the older man, who I was starting to think might be a chief of some kind.

I ought to mention that these men weren't dressed for war. There were no paint-striped faces, no decorative shields or feathered bonnets. They wore mostly buckskins and moccasins, although a few of them had on cloth shirts. Several wore revolvers, as well—something else you don't see in those moving-picture shows.

The younger man spoke to the older man, then all eyes shifted to me. A chill, like a chunk of ice dropped down your shirt on a hot day, skittered crookedly along my spine. Looking at the younger warrior who was doing all the talking, something suddenly clicked in my mind. It didn't take long for me to figure out what it was, my experience with Indians being limited to the extreme in those days.

"Hey, I know him," I blurted, then immediately wished I could reel those words back into my mouth. They'd all heard me, and I feared I'd committed some kind of taboo by speaking without being spoken to first, that being the white-eyed practice I'd been raised on. The younger Indian eyed me for a moment, then spoke again to the older man.

If you're wondering where I'd seen that Indian before, it was the preceding year, in the spring of 1878. I'd just taken Syd's cattle into the high country for the summer, and was on my way back. I'd stopped for the night in a grove of aspens along a pretty little stream to fix my supper, which was a rabbit I'd shot earlier, along with some rice and raisins, a concoction the trail cooks called spotted pup, when I became aware of someone standing across the fire from me.

Yup, it was the very same Indian who was talking to the elderly warrior now. He was a well-put-together fellow in leggings and a scarlet breechcloth. A heavy knife rode in a sheath on his hip, and he was carrying an old Hudson's Bay trade musket with its barrel cut down to make it easier to handle from the back of a horse. He hadn't been pointing the musket at me that night below the Black Pines, but he'd been holding it in both hands like he was ready to use if he had to.

There are a lot of wrong moves you can make when an enemy walks into your camp unannounced, and make no mistake about it, we were enemies. The recent Bannock War was too fresh in both of our memories to consider ourselves anything but a threat to one another. Fact is, I don't know why he didn't just shoot me from the darkness. It would have made things a lot simpler for him.

That night back below the Black Pines, this Indian—he was wearing an owl's feather in his hair, so in my mind, I'd already dubbed him Owl—was looking both footsore and hungry. Without thinking about the consequences, I made a careful motion toward the rabbit, skewered above the low flames of my fire, and said: "Care to eat?"

Owl stared at me for almost a full minute, as if measuring the sincerity of my invitation. I didn't say a word, and I sure as heck didn't make any sudden moves. The air around the fire that night was so hair-trigger tense I figured even a sneeze could have set us both off.

After pondering on it for a spell, Owl shifted the musket to his left hand and strode into camp. He squatted down across from me and reached for the rabbit. He could have eaten it all and I wouldn't have said anything, but instead he tore it down the middle and gave me the bigger half. We stripped that rabbit down to the bone, me and him sitting there wound up like a couple of mandolin strings, the fire cracking and popping between us.

After we finished the rabbit, I fetched my kettle of spotted pup off the fire and dished a noticeably larger half onto a plate and handed it to Owl. He took it with a stoic expression, although I thought I detected a hint of amusement in his eyes. We cleaned that pup up slick as a whistle, and, when he was finished, Owl set the plate on the ground and stood.

Not sure how to respond, I remained seated. Speaking nary a word the whole time, Owl slowly faded back into the darkness. I'll tell you, it was spooky the way he didn't even look to see where he was going or where he placed his feet. For a brief moment I wondered if maybe he'd been a ghost, but then I reasoned that ghosts likely didn't eat real food. Not to mention that Hudson's Bay *fuzee* had sure looked real enough.

Now here I was, staring at that same man once more, only there wasn't any hint of amusement in his eyes today. Wasn't none of 'em breaking a smile, for that matter, and I ain't ashamed to say my scalp was crawling.

Owl—he was still wearing his feather—and the chief confabbed for several minutes while the others looked on with growing discontent. It seemed obvious they didn't care for the direction the conversation was taking. From time to time one of them would bust in on them, but the chief largely ignored their interruptions and focused on what Owl was telling him. After a bit, he spoke a few words, and Owl nodded and kicked his buckskin forward.

Beside me, McCandles said: "Kid, I hope to h--- you know what you're doing."

"You just sit tight and keep your mouth shut," I replied, cramming as much confidence into my voice as my fear would allow.

Owl drew up a few yards away. "I know you, as well," he said, speaking better English than a lot of white-eyes I knew. "Now it is my turn to return a favor. I had lost my horse the last time I saw you, and my musket was empty. You gave me food to ease the hunger in my belly. For that, I now give you your life, even though there are others here who want your horses and guns." His gaze shifted deliberately to the women. He didn't say anything about them, and I reckon he didn't have to. From her rear seat on the palomino, Della was muttering a curse-infested prayer.

What came out of me next likely saved my life, although I don't know where it came from. I sure hadn't planned on saying it.

"Maybe you and your friends can still get some guns and horses," I said.

Ian gave me a sharp look.

"We are being followed by men who have many guns," I went on.

McCandles swore softly. "You god d---ed traitor."

Owl's gaze shifted between us, lingered briefly on McCandles's bound wrists and puffy fingers, then came back to me. "He is your prisoner?"

I nodded. "He killed a man who was like a father to me. I'm taking him back to hang for his crime."

Owl seemed to flinch at the word *hang*. I found out later that a lot of Indians consider that particular form of execution especially vile. Something about the rope closing off the throat so that a person's spirit couldn't escape to fly up to the Happy Hunting Grounds or something.

"You should leave now," Owl said stonily. "You should never come back. My debt to you is paid. The next time I see you, I might want to kill you."

That was good enough for me, and I reined Hammerhead around without so much as a good bye and told Lucy to scoot. The Indians disappeared as soon as we rounded the first bend, but my scalp didn't stop wiggling for hours.

SESSION EIGHT

I got to wondering last night if you had enough of those plastic cylinder things to record on. Nobody's ever asked me for so much detail before, and I didn't think it would take this long to tell my story. Shoot, I wasn't even sure I'd *remember* all of these details. It's been kind of fun the way it's all come back to me.

Anyway, after our run-in with the Bannocks, McCandles's demeanor changed drastically. He'd barely speak, even at night when I'd hitch him to a tree or a stump or something else he wasn't likely to pick up and run away with. The truth is, he was starting to look a little peaked. He didn't cuss or complain or even make threats about what he intended to do to me once he got free. It was a blessed silence for my part, but worrisome, too. Me and Lucy both figured he was cooking up something devious.

Della wasn't talking much, either, although that could have been because she was exhausted. I don't know if I mentioned this earlier, but Della Wilson was no spring chicken. Back in the gulch she'd done what she could to make herself attractive, but what little powder she'd had had all been scrubbed off on the long ride out of there. She was looking frazzled on every side now, her hair a wild tangle that reminded me of freshly rusted wire, and the pouches under her eyes were dark enough to give her a raccoon-like appearance. She was sore all over, and having aged considerably myself since then, I can appreciate how she must have felt. Especially her rump. A hard-seated saddle like we all rode in those days was damaging enough, but riding the leather skirt behind the cantle must have been pure torture. She never griped about it, though. I don't know why, because she complained about other things all the time. But I could tell it was wearing her down.

Lucy wasn't doing a whole lot better. She looked drained to the point of lethargy, and was in about the same condition as Della, tailbone-wise. Watching her from a distance, you'd swear you were staring at a seventy-year-old washerwoman. In my opinion, Lucy had it worse than the rest of us, having to ride her sorrel bareback like she did. Stirrups make a big difference after a while.

As for me, tired doesn't begin to describe what I was feeling. I was running on pure adrenaline by then, and knew that, when I finally was able to let go, I'd collapse like an empty gunny sack. I was constantly cold and always hungry, and the muscles of my inner thighs felt like they were being sliced by razors every time I dropped from the gray's saddle. I do believe I ached in every muscle and joint in my body, and I was just a kid back then, in pretty good condition.

I was also stubborn, and that's never really changed. I mentioned yesterday that I'd become so determined to see Mc-Candles hang for Syd's murder that I was willing to risk my own neck, along with Lucy's and Della's, to see him brought to trial. I never again wavered from that decision.

We finally got down out of the mountains, free of the criss-crossing ridges and shallow cañons, and came to a stream called Goose Creek. I'd crossed this very same stretch of water on my way to the gulch, but hadn't known its name. Lucy told it to me now, explaining that it had been one of McCandles's men, Ben Ryder, whose sorrel horse she was now riding, who had revealed the stream's identity to her. She admitted that she hadn't cared at the time, and it didn't mean much to me, either, other than that it can be a comfort to have an idea of where you are in the world. That's a big, empty land out there, and it still is. A body can feel almighty small creeping across it, so even something as simple as a name can make it seem a bit less intimidating.

We camped that night in a grove of cottonwoods along the Goose, and for once we had all the water we needed. I picketed the horses on the lush grass growing along the creek's banks, and left them to graze. When I got back to camp, I discovered that Lucy and Della were gone. Before I could start to worry, I heard a splash from the river, followed by an in-drawn curse from Della that must have turned the air around her blue for at least half a dozen feet. I grinned, picturing her doughy white body change into a similar shade of sapphire. I'd bellied down earlier for a drink, and found the water cold enough to make my teeth hurt.

McCandles lay where I'd dropped him, his eyes closed, although I could tell he wasn't asleep. It irritated me that Lucy had been lured away, leaving him unguarded. I went over to nudge his foot, just to check. "You still alive?"

McCandles didn't reply. He barely raised his head. It was the look in his eyes that told me there was still plenty of life left in him. Trouble, too, I figured.

I started to walk away, but then I stopped and turned. I don't know why, but for the longest time I just stared at him, and after a while an unfamiliar feeling began to come over me. Not exactly anger, but a kind of fed-up-ed-ness, if that's even a real expression.

McCandles returned my stare, and it suddenly dawned on me how tired I was of being treated like dirt, like some half-witted kid who had achieved what he had only through dumb luck. My face grew warm and my eyes narrowed until it was like I was looking down a long tube, with McCandles's sneering face at the other end. I don't know what made me do it, or

131

what I hoped to accomplish by it, but I slowly drew the Colt from my holster and pointed it at McCandles.

He frowned as I rocked the hammer back with deliberate slowness. My finger tightened on the trigger, easing the tension off the main spring. Just one more speck of pressure and McCandles would be dead. I knew it. He knew it, and his eyes widened until I finally saw what I longed to see. Ian McCandles was frightened. No, he was terrified. He thought I was going to exert that last bit of pull and blow his head to a bloody pulp. And to tell you the truth, when I look back on that moment, I'm kind of surprised that I didn't. For whatever reason, for those few brief seconds, it was like I'd stepped outside of my body, leaving the mechanisms of bone and muscle to act on the most basic of primitive instincts—to kill the son-of-a-b---- who had caused me so much grief, who had murdered probably the only real friend I had in the world, then kidnapped and abused the only woman I'd ever cared about.

I remember thinking: *Why am I going to so much trouble to let someone else do what needs to be done?*

Kill him now, I thought, *before something happens to prevent it from happening.*

What if McCandles had managed to escape that afternoon? What if those Bannocks had killed me but failed to stop the man I was hauling to an uncertain justice? What if a good lawyer got him off altogether? I didn't have any proof that it was Ian who had actually shot Syd, or if he'd even drawn his gun.

And the biggest if of all: what if his gang beat us to City of Rocks? What if some of them were already there, waiting for us? McCandles would go free, and everything I'd endured, everything I'd risked to bring him back, would be for naught. I'd be just another set of bones left to feed the wolves—assuming the vultures didn't get me first.

And then, with all these thoughts bouncing around in my

brain, I lowered the hammer and holstered the Colt.

I thought McCandles was going to weep, which goes to show you what kind of stress he was under. I studied him quietly for another minute—his hands puffed up obscenely from lack of circulation, his whole left leg now swollen from where I'd busted his knee. I felt no sympathy for him. What I wanted to feel was contempt, but I couldn't even manage that. Finally I turned away to kindle a fire, and McCandles fell back and closed his eyes. By the time the women returned, their faces scrubbed clean, their hair washed and finger-combed, I already had the coffee brewing.

We continued down Goose Creek all the following day, making our way steadily northward. I kept the group moving at a good clip, even though it was taking its toll on the horses—Syd's palomino in particular. That flaxen-maned beast was as pretty a horse as you were likely to come across in that part of Idaho, but on the trail it was proving to lack the stamina of even my runty little gray. Hammerhead just kept on chugging, although he was losing weight like the rest of them.

I'd stop the group from time to time and climb a nearby ridge or knoll to check our back trail, but there was never anything to see. Not even a cloud of dust on the horizon. It gnawed on me not to know what had become of our pursuers. I wondered how would I feel if I later found out Owl's warriors had set a trap for them, maybe even killed them. I'd be as guilty of their murder as the Bannocks, yet I knew I'd do no less if they caught up with us. I would have to kill them if I didn't want to die the slow death McCandles kept promising me.

We made a fireless camp well back from the trail that night, and Lucy served us a meal of cold rice and beans left over from the day before, poor repast by anyone's standards. After making sure McCandles and Della were securely bedded down, I took my blanket and walked off about twenty yards to sit with my back against a low dirt bank where I could keep an eye on both the camp and the creek. I kept my gun belt buckled, and placed the Evans across my lap. I intended to be ready in case the Mc-Candles gang showed up after dark, but it didn't work out that way. I closed my eyes against the dusty feel of their sockets, and, when I next opened them, dawn was carving crimson slashes in the eastern sky.

Before it grew too light, I had Lucy build a fire and fix a warm breakfast. She brewed coffee and made biscuits with the last of our flour. Her expression drew taut as she rummaged through the grub sack.

"Maybe two more pots of coffee, no more than that of rice, and there ain't enough beans left for a full meal. There's not going to be enough food for all of us," she said.

"We'll have to make do."

"Just that easy, huh?"

"I've seen a few ducks along the creek. I can shoot one of them, and maybe we'll run across a deer or an elk that I can put a sneak on."

"I haven't seen any ducks since we turned north, and we're moving too fast to hunt deer or elk. They'd probably hear us coming from a mile away."

"She's right," McCandles piped in from the far side of the fire. "It's going to be slim pickings real soon."

"You mind your own beeswax," I told him. "If we've got to cut rations, you'll be the first one I quit feeding."

McCandles chuckled, his old, antagonistic self creeping back out of the grave where his aches and pains had tried to bury it. I wondered if it was our encounter the night before that had him trying to reclaim his manhood.

"How are you going to find all that gold if I'm too weak to take you there?" he asked.

"I'd like to take that gold back to Coalville, but it ain't my number one priority," I said.

"I want the gold," Lucy said bluntly. She was staring hard. "I've been thinking about this a lot, Joey. The money's already been taken. It's not like we were the ones stealing it."

Della had been reclining next to the fire. She sat up now, a fresh spark of interest rallying her features.

"Even if they know who robbed the stage, they wouldn't come after us," Lucy said. "They'll be looking for Ian's men."

"Ian would just spill the beans the minute we got back to civilization," I told her.

"I wouldn't if we split the money between us," McCandles said, leaning forward. "You take your share and go wherever you want. I'll take mine and head in the opposite direction."

"You mean, *we'll* head in the opposite direction," Della said.

McCandles grinned. "Why, sure, honey, that's what I meant. You and me."

"Uhn-uh." I shook my head. "You're going to Coalville to stand trial for murder, McCandles, and the money will go back to whoever you stole it from."

"Joey, that money could get us out of Coalville . . . for good," Lucy said. "Don't you want to live some place bigger and brighter, where there ain't rattlesnakes under the floorboards and rats in the cabinets?"

"You could come to San Francisco with me and Della, kid," McCandles offered. "H---, with that kind of money, you could go to Paris."

"I didn't lose anything in Paris, or San Francisco," I replied.

"If you don't want it, give your share back, but don't kill my dreams, too," Lucy said. "Please, Joey. I'm never gonna get another chance like this."

"It's stealing, Lucy."

"I didn't steal it. Ian did."

I wanted to tell her that it would be the same thing, but the

135

words seemed to jam up in my throat. I guess I'd known ever since talking to her that first time in the gulch that her only concern was for getting out of this mess alive, and to h--- with my noble rescue effort or justice for poor Ruby Davidson and Syd Hackett. I won't deny that a certain part of me was disappointed in her for that, even if I could understand it, which I did. But this wasn't survival, it was greed, and it revealed an ugliness that I'd never seen in her before. I think that's why I've come to despise avarice so much. Every time I hear of a politician taking money or gifts from a lobbyist, or switching tracks on some proposition in order to give a wealthy businessman a little more opportunity at taxpayer expense, I see Lucy's face on that morning above Goose Creek, and the word that pops into my mind is: whore.

I felt something crumble inside of me. I couldn't have named it then, but I think now I'd call it the last vestiges of my belief in good versus evil. I don't know if that makes sense to you or not. I just know that my feelings were tangled up in a web of disenchantment that I'd first experienced only a week before, in a darkened café in Coalville. And now I was getting slammed over the head with it a second time. After everything Ian McCandles had subjected her to, had done to her, Lucy Lytle was still willing to throw in with him for a share of a box of gold. I'll tell you, it made me about half sick to my stomach.

"No," I said after a lengthy silence. "The money goes to Coalville, same as McCandles."

Lucy stiffened. I thought for a minute she was going to say something else, but then she abruptly spun on the balls of her feet and walked away. I watched until she disappeared into the tall sage, then turned back to the fire. Della had laid back, the hope in her eyes like extinguished candles. Only McCandles seemed unfazed. He lay on his side with the saddle in front of him, that taut little grin that I'd come to despise so much back on his stubbled face.

"You're taking a lot onto yourself, kid," he said.

"I told you to shut up."

"I heard you the first time." For a moment I thought he was going to say more, but then he just chuckled pleasantly, the way you do when someone tells you a joke that is kind of funny, but not hilarious.

In a funk, I squatted next to the fire and poked some limbs into the low flames. The coffee was ready and I poured myself a cup but didn't offer any to the others. Della seemed immune to the aroma wafting from the pot—probably too sore to notice—but McCandles said: "How about a cup of that java to ease the chill?"

"Wait your turn," I replied.

There was that smile again, quick and pointed, like he knew something I didn't. Holding out his hands, he said: "I could help myself if you'd cut me loose like you did Della."

"That ain't likely."

McCandles's smile faded. "I ain't hardly been able to feel my fingers for a couple of days now. I'd hate to lose them because you're scared."

"Who said I was scared?"

He pushed his hands forward once more. "Then cut me loose, at least until I get some feeling back in my paws."

"No."

"Oh, for Christ's sake!" Della cried. "Cut him loose, Roper. He's too crippled to run, and, if you let gangrene take his fingers, you'll be no better than you claim he is."

Now, that was a new thought, and one I should have come to myself. I scowled as I blew across the top of my coffee to cool it. I didn't like McCandles. H---, at that moment, I didn't much care for any of them. But the more I thought about it, the more I realized Della was right.

Setting my cup aside, I walked over to where McCandles was propped against his saddle. I said: "If you try anything, if you so much as twitch, I'm going to put a bullet through that other knee of yours. You savvy?"

McCandles bit his lip to keep from responding. I can only imagine what he wanted to say, but I doubt it would have been pretty. Bending forward, I untied the knots securing his wrists, then stepped back and put my hand on the Colt. But McCandles only moaned as he slowly straightened his limbs. His fingers looked purple in the chilly light, and I hoped I hadn't waited too long.

Della sat up. "You want me to rub them hands for you, sweetie?"

McCandles nodded, his face pinched in agony as he tried unsuccessfully to flex his fingers. Scooting over to his side, Della began massaging his hands and wrists. I backed off and picked up the Evans. I wasn't taking any chances.

I gave them half an hour. When Lucy came back, I could tell she had been crying, but I didn't care. I told her to saddle the horses, then ordered Della to break camp. While they did that, I sat across from McCandles, just staring at him like I didn't give a d--- one way or another, which by then was getting pretty close to the truth.

With the horses readied, I had Della help McCandles into the saddle. His left leg was nearly useless at that point, barely able to support his weight even with assistance. When he was mounted, I had Lucy moor his wrists to the saddle horn. She shot me a dark look, but did what she was told. When she finished, I leaned the Evans against the bank to double check her knots.

"Are you on his side now?" I asked.

"It's tight enough. Are you trying to cripple him?"

"Me and him's already had that conversation this morning,"

I told her, snugging up her only semi-snug hitch.

Fetching my rifle, I swung a leg over my saddle and told the others to mount.

We rode back to Goose Creek, then turned north again, still following the right-hand bank. I knew we were getting close to City of Rocks, but I wasn't sure of its exact location. Pulling the palomino up alongside the gray, I said: "I'm flat out of patience, McCandles, so tell me the quickest way to City of Rocks from here."

He looked up, licking his lips thoughtfully, calculating his answer. I released the Evans' safety, then let the muzzle swing over against his right knee.

"That way," he said, indicating a northwesterly direction with a tip of his head.

"How far?"

"I can't be sure, but I doubt if it's more than another day or two."

I pressed the Evans' muzzle tighter against his kneecap. "You know what I'm going to do if you're lying to me, don't you?"

He considered my threat for a minute, then said: "Maybe it's more east than west. Over that ridge yonder."

I couldn't help smiling. A few days ago he would have cursed me for my question, and never considered backing down from a lie. I think he was finally starting to recognize the grim reality of my determination.

"How far?"

After another drawn-out hesitation, he said: "Half a day to the southern edge of the Rocks. Another half to where we're going. We won't make it tonight, but we'll be close."

I nodded, satisfied he was telling the truth. "Let's make some tracks," I said, and we reined away from Goose Creek for the last time.

That afternoon, Lucy volunteered to take over leading the

palomino. I accepted her offer. Maybe it was foolish of me, especially with her riding bareback and not having anything to grab if the palomino balked or tried to bolt, but I liked the idea of having everyone out in front of me for a change. Even Lucy. What little trust in her I'd had after she pulled the Colt on me the other day had evaporated completely that morning.

I let the three of them pull ahead by about thirty feet, then heeled the gray after them. I heard them talking back and forth a few times, but not much, and nothing that seemed to include me, so I let it slide.

As luck would have it, we came to a trail that took us over the high ridge McCandles had pointed out that morning. It was steep and treacherous in places, and we paused on top to let our animals blow. It was there that I got my first good look at City of Rocks, way off in the distance.

Man, that is a wildly beautiful country, as breathtaking from a distance as it is up close. If you've never been there, you ought to go. I won't, not ever again, but that's only because of my history with the place.

There were rocks everywhere, and I don't mean the gravelly kind. I'm talking about towering stone pillars, fluted slabs, and jutting bluffs. Between the patches of gray rocks were grassy vales scored by icy brooks. Piñon trees, some of the tallest I've ever seen, offered good shade and firewood. I saw bighorn sheep up on some of the higher peaks, and deer and elk sign was plentiful. Late in the afternoon we crossed the trail of a mammoth grizzly bear, its lingering scent nearly setting the horses into a fit of pitching. Eyeballing the size of those prints, I could appreciate the horses' fear. I don't believe I'm exaggerating when I say I could have placed my foot in a single track and had room to spare on every side.

It was after dark by the time we wound our way far enough into the stony metropolis to feel like we'd arrived. Coming to a broad valley, I had Lucy take a bead on a stand of piñons near its center, and we made our camp there.

I felt safe enough in the location to have Della build a fire, then put together a skimpy supper while Lucy saw to the horses. I found a spot about twenty yards away and sat back with the Evans across my lap. I wasn't as worried about food tonight as I had been that morning, and felt fairly confident that I could slip up on something edible tomorrow. I figured even a small deer would afford us enough meat to last us to Coalville.

It was a pretty night. Stars freckled the sky, and the moon was just coming up like a blister on dark skin. It was breezy, though, and I was glad to have my heavy coat. It would have been warmer down by the fire, but I wasn't craving company, and I could see that Della and McCandles—and Lucy, when she got back—were in a chatty mood. I probably should have gone down and told them to shut up, but I was growing weary of always having to be on top of every situation. Unfortunately remaining seated was a decision I'd soon come to regret.

Lucy brought me my supper—a couple of leftover biscuits and a half cup of weak coffee. She handed them to me silently, then turned back toward camp.

"You still mad at me?" I asked.

She stopped, but it was several heartbeats before she turned around. "You're just a kid, Joey. You don't understand what that kind of money could mean to someone like me."

"It's not your money."

"So you've said."

"There's more to life than being rich."

"You can say that, living like you do? A shack behind the livery, the laughingstock of the whole town?"

"I ain't heard nobody laughing," I fired back. My position in Coalville's hierarchy was a touchy subject for me.

"You're an idiot, Joe Roper. Someday, you'll figure that out."

I watched her walk away, my protest unspoken. Eventually I would recognize the truth of her words, but that night I just sat there, numbed by her accusation. It was a long time before I fell asleep. When I awoke the next morning, everything was gone. Even the horses.

SESSION NINE

Right now you're probably saying to yourself what a fool I'd been to lower my guard like that, and you'd be right. I realized it myself as soon as I saw the deserted camp.

It was all gone—food, saddles, blankets, everything. Only the ashes from last night's fire remained, and they were cold to the touch, telling me they had pulled out early, probably before midnight.

Two things puzzled me. One was that I still had both of my guns—the Evans and the nickeled Colt I'd confiscated from McCandles. The other was the fact that I was still alive. That had to be Lucy's doing. She'd held some kind of trump card over the others and had used it to spare my life, because I knew as sure as the sun was about to crest the horizon that, if it had been up to McCandles, I'd have been spitted above a roasting fire to die that slow death he'd been promising me.

I tried to sort out the sign they'd left behind, but it was a jumble. The iron-shod prints of our horses were everywhere, in and around the trees, out on pasture, and the farther I ranged from camp, the skimpier and more difficult it became. Finally giving up on the idea of tracking them, I rolled my blanket into a tight bundle and slung it over my shoulder along with the Evans. Then I headed for the highest point I could see, a jutting pinnacle that looked like it was trying to thumb a ride with the swiftly moving clouds overhead.

I've heard that people go to City of Rocks nowadays to try

their hand at rock climbing. If they're looking for a challenge, I'd say they've chosen well. I circled that stone pillar—it must have been forty feet in diameter and half again as tall—twice before deciding on a crumbling ledge that looked like it might take me to the top. After scrutinizing the area around me and judging myself alone, I set my guns and blanket aside, draped my heavy coat over it all, then set out for an eagle's-eye view of the surrounding terrain.

I hadn't climbed ten feet when I began to sweat, and I'm not talking about from the physical exertion. That ledge was so narrow I couldn't get my feet entirely on it. If not for the random handholds I kept finding as I crept upward, I would have been forced back to the ground before I'd barely made my start. By the time I reached twenty-five feet, I was beginning to wish the handholds *would* peter out. At least that way I'd have an excuse to abandon the climb. But every time I was about to give up, I'd spot another crevice to wiggle my fingers into, allowing me to crawl upward another few inches.

After thirty feet, I quit looking down. I was cursing steadily under my breath, a habit I've had for as long as I can remember—swearing softly every time I'd find myself in a dangerous situation, as if an unbroken stream of profanity could take my mind off the risks.

Save for ten skinned knuckles and a couple of bruised shins, I made it to the top in one piece. As soon as I got there, I belly-crawled to the center of the monolith's cap, then sprawled out to wait for my heart to slow its patter and for the breeze to dry the sweat on my brow. Even on a table top surface as broad and nearly as flat as this one was, I didn't want to stand up. In the back of my mind was the knowledge that, very soon, I was going to have to climb back down, and the prospect terrified me.

But I couldn't lie there forever, so after a few minutes I cautiously rose to my feet to have a look around.

I'll tell you what—I know now why people want to climb mountains. Staring out across the country from the top of that pinnacle was one of the most wondrous occurrences of my life. H--- will freeze over before I ever do it again, but I'm glad I got to experience it once. The view was spectacular, and it wasn't long before I began easing forward for a better look.

What I saw when I got to the edge nearly took my breath away. And no, it wasn't the scenery. Apparently Lucy, Della, and McCandles hadn't made much progress after leaving me behind. Maybe they'd gotten lost in the dark or confused by the maze of rocks, but I don't think they were more than three or four miles away from where I now stood, at least as the crow flies.

Easing up to the very lip of the drop-off, I studied the terrain that separated us. From this height, it wasn't hard to pick out a route that would put me right behind them within a matter of hours, assuming I pushed myself and they continued the sauntering pace they seemed to be maintaining now. With luck, I could catch up before dusk.

Trouble was, the city's population had grown overnight. My eyes were drawn to the west, where another group of horsemen had appeared several miles away, angling toward the center of the range. I counted five of them, and, while I couldn't be absolutely certain from here, I figured the odds were good that they were a part of the McCandles gang. What was worse was, if they continued their current course, they would likely catch up with Lucy and the others before I did.

Climbing down off that pinnacle was a lot harder than going up, primarily because in looking for a place to grab onto with my hands or feet, I had to look down. Sixty feet might not seem like a lot when you're sitting at a table talking about it, but from up top, it's a whole different perspective.

Well, I made it, and still in one piece, although my arms were trembling badly. I took a couple of minutes to compose myself, then put on my coat and buckled the gun belt around my waist. I'd have to leave my blanket behind. Without a piece of rope or a leather thong to tie it into a bundle, it would be too difficult to carry, and I needed to make tracks if I wanted to catch up with Lucy and them before those other fellows did.

I made good time, having already scouted my route from above. I'd jog a ways, then walk long enough to catch my breath, then pick up the pace again. As rough as that country is, it took me nearly two hours to reach the spot where I'd earlier seen my quarry. They'd naturally moved on, but luck was on my side, because I finally located a line of hoof prints clear enough for me to follow.

I dogged their trail all morning and into the afternoon, but I finally had to stop when I came to a small spring where they had paused to water their horses. My calves and hamstrings were aching something fierce, and I was feeling light-headed from hunger. After a drink, I flopped in the shade with my legs splayed out before me. It was maybe twenty minutes later—I hadn't moved a muscle the whole time—when several does and a young buck deer darted out of the trees below me. Instantly alert, I rolled into some nearby bushes. A few minutes later the horsemen I'd spotted from the top of the pinnacle rode past, no more than thirty yards away.

I recognized all five of them from that night in the Palace. Ben Ryder, whose sorrel I'd stolen from behind Della's cabin in the gulch, was there astride a black filly. Jud Linderman was also there. The two of them stepped down to stretch their legs while their horses drank. Hooking a knee around his saddle horn, Reuben Stanton pulled the makings from a vest pocket and began to roll a cigarette, while Carl Baily, wearing a blood-stained bandage above his left wrist, fished a strip of jerky from his saddlebags.

After allowing his mount only a few quick swallows, Yakima Tom Candy jerked the horse's head up and spurred it across the stream that flowed for about fifty yards down into the small valley below where I laid curled up like a woolly worm. Yakima rode up and down the opposite bank until he spotted the tracks Lucy, Della, and McCandles had left behind, then reined onto their trail.

His voice as clear as if he was standing over me, Ben Ryder said: "You reckon that crazy-eyed son-of-a-b---- found something?"

"Looks like it," Jud replied. Then he and Ben swung their legs over their saddles and rode after the half-breed. Reuben had already crossed the stream to follow Yakima, his cigarette dangling from the corner of his mouth like spittle. Only Carl Baily lingered, squinting uphill after the others as if debating whether or not he wanted to continue. When Jud reined in about forty yards up the side of the ridge, Ben hauled up beside him.

"I reckon it's them, all right!" Jud called back to Carl.

Carl folded a strip of jerky into his mouth, then nudged his horse across the stream. Coming alongside Jud's bay, he leaned from his saddle to study the tracks. When he straightened, there was a big grin on his face. "They're fresh," he said, his voice carrying easily to my hiding place in the bushes at the head of the spring.

"D---ed right they're fresh," Reuben said. "Let's ride, boys. I aim to catch up with that gutless wonder before dark." He kicked his horse after Yakima, but the others held back.

"I do believe ol' Reuben is more intent on killing McCandles than he is on finding our gold," Jud observed.

"He can have all four of 'em if that's what he wants," Ben said, not realizing I was no longer a part of the group. "All I want is my share of the loot."

147

Then the three of them rode off after Reuben and Yakima, climbing to the top of the ridge before turning north.

As soon as they were gone, I slipped out from under my bush. For a while I just stood there, staring at the ridge where the outlaws had disappeared. Then I moseyed over to take another long drink from the spring. I gave the horsemen twenty minutes to put some distance between us, then set out on their trail.

Looking for a silver lining, I finally settled on the notion that having the whole of McCandles's gang in front of me, or at least what there was of it—there were still a couple of members unaccounted for—would make it somewhat more convenient for me, as I wouldn't have to worry about them coming up on me from behind.

Unfortunately that was the only advantage I could see. Everything else just seemed to darken my prospects. Not only had the odds jumped radically out of my favor—you know, assuming they had ever really been in my favor—but now I also had to worry that the addition of the five hardcases would complicate matters in ways I couldn't yet begin to imagine.

For instance, if what Jud Linderman had said about Reuben Stanton being more interested in revenge than on recovering the gold, how would that effect my recapture of McCandles? I wanted Ian alive, at least until he could be hung legally. I sure didn't want to see him shot down by one of his own men for a perceived double-cross. And what would I do about Lucy and Della if the McCandles gang caught up with them? Did I still want to rescue them? Would they even want to be rescued?

Part of me was wishing that I hadn't decided to go after the stashed booty, although I was logical enough to realize that Mc-Candles's men would have probably caught up with us no matter which direction we fled.

As the day wore on, the trail took an increasingly rugged

bent, leaving the ridge tops for miles at a time to flounder across the lower slopes. It wound around huge boulders, through dense stands of buckbrush and piñons, and across streams that could have been more easily forded elsewhere. At one point it rolled down a slope so steep it's a wonder I didn't find someone dead at the bottom.

After a while I began to wonder if this wasn't McCandles's way of slowing the women down long enough for his men to catch up, which would be puzzling, if true. Didn't he know what they thought of him? That Reuben Stanton, at least, wanted him dead?

One thing their roundabout course did seem to imply to me was that McCandles was still a prisoner. Lucy's prisoner. That had to be the trump card she'd held over him last night, and why I was still alive today. Nothing else made sense.

As crazy as it might sound, I felt a moment of pride for her. She knew, probably better than me, that, if McCandles ever did get free, he'd be just as likely to shoot both her and Della as help them. She also had to be aware that he would never share the gold with them, no matter what promises he might make along the way. It made me smile to visualize her command of the little group, especially Ian's seething anger, for I knew the gunman well enough by now to know that he would be contemplating Lucy's torturous death as vividly as he once had mine.

I kept up as swift a pace as I could manage over such unforgiving terrain. Sweat was rolling down my face in rivulets, darkening my shirt in front and back and under my arms. My feet and legs screamed. There were times when I wondered if I wasn't crippling myself in my rush to catch up, but I wouldn't quit. I don't think I could've quit any more. Pursuit had been branded into my brain.

I was keeping a sharp eye out in front of me as I jogged along because I didn't want to blunder into anyone. I should have been watching in every direction. I was traveling a ridge-top trail through some twisted piñons when a voice behind me snapped: "Throw your hands up, bub, or I'm gonna plug you where you stand."

That's what he said, that he'd *plug me*. I'd never heard the expression before, and I wouldn't hear it again until some years ago in, I think, a Tom Mix movie. But I'll tell you what, even after all those years, those words uttered against ol' Tom made my flesh crawl.

I froze up solid until the guy behind me said: "Get rid of that rifle."

I tossed the Evans off to the side, where it skidded downslope about a dozen feet.

"Turn around."

I did as I was told, and a burly man with a bloody rag wrapped around his left wrist stepped out of the shadows of a tall piñon. It was Carl Baily, and he was holding a Smith & Wesson Schofield revolver pointed straight at my belly.

"You know, I've got to learn to trust that half-breed son-of-a-b----," Carl said. He sounded pleasantly surprised by our encounter. "Yakima said you were watching us back at that stream where we watered our horses, but I didn't believe him. H---, the only reason I hung back was to prove him wrong. Now look what I caught." He made a motion with the Smith & Wesson. "Unbuckle that rig from around your waist and toss it over here."

Still alive and wanting to keep it that way, I quickly shucked McCandles's gun belt.

"Over here," Carl repeated, and I sent it arching across the twenty or so feet that separated us. It landed at Carl's feet, kicking up a cloud of dust and dried piñon needles.

"You know, I always did admire this *pistola*," Carl said, nudging the tooled leather holster with a toe. "I might just swap it for my own. Sure as h---, McCandles ain't gonna need it where Yakima Tom and Reuben Stanton intend to send him."

So far, I hadn't opened my mouth. I didn't see a reason to start now. Carl bent forward to pick up McCandles's belt. As he did, the nickeled Colt started to slide from its bucket.

I reckon it must have been jolted loose when it hit the ground, because it wasn't a slicked-up rig like the movie cowboys wear. Anyway, when McCandles's revolver started to slip out, Carl instinctively grabbed for it with his other hand, the one holding the Smith & Wesson.

That was my chance, and I took it without contemplation. With Carl's attention momentarily diverted, I plunged off that ridge-top trail like a leaping buck to go skittering recklessly down a gully that twisted and buckled toward a meadow a couple of hundred feet below.

Carl hollered for me to stop, but I kept on jack-rabbiting downhill as fast as my legs could carry me. Carl immediately opened fire, and I had bullets slicing the air on either side of me. Throwing a glance over my shoulder, I saw him coming after me, shooting as he ran. Likely that's what saved my bacon that day. I don't care how good a pistol shot you are, I don't think there's a shooter alive—man, woman, or child—who can come close to a target while running downhill in slick-soled boots.

Being younger and faster, I was rapidly increasing the distance between us. Enough so that, when he stopped to reload, I managed to duck out of sight, then scramble over the top of that gully on my hands and knees and drop into the next one. I was pretty sure I hadn't been seen.

Remember how I described the way most mountain ranges ran like fingers coming down off the top of your hand—ridges and gullies coming down off of more ridges and gullies—a regular lattice of broken country separating mountain top and valley floor? Once I managed to get over the top of that smaller ridge, I immediately switched directions and began climbing back toward where Carl had first waylaid me. I could hear him coming down the neighboring gulch like a drunken goose, bouncing into trees and stumbling through the low brush, all the while shouting for me to stop running and take my medicine. Naturally I kept climbing.

At one point silence drifted over the mountainside, and I sank down behind a large rock jutting from the side of the mountain. I heard Carl say: "I've got you in my sights now, bub. You'd better come on out or I'll shoot you where you stand."

I flinched at his words, but it took me only a moment to realize he was bluffing. He had no idea where I was, and after a few seconds I started climbing again, though trying my best to be quiet about it.

Even with that, I must have made some little noise. Or maybe it was just poor luck. Whatever the reason, I hadn't gained more than a few feet when Carl appeared over the lip of the same gully I was using. He spotted me right off and snapped a shot at me that came close enough to kick dirt over the heels of my shoes. He kept shooting, too, but I had forty or fifty feet on him by now, and I made the most of it.

I was badly winded by the time I reached the top. Sucking in ragged drafts of cool mountain air, I began scanning the slope for the Evans. Carl kept firing, and as he drew nearer his bullets started coming closer to where I was pacing back and forth like a steel target in a shooting gallery. Likely I should have kept on running, but my concentration was too caught up in locating my rifle to think of other options.

Carl was less than twenty-five feet away when I finally spotted the Evans, half hidden under a low hanging piñon bough. I dived for the rifle just as Carl leveled his Smith & Wesson and pulled the trigger. I figured I was a dead man at that point, so I think I was as surprised as he was when the Smith & Wesson's hammer fell with a cold snap on a dead chamber. Turns out he'd shot the piece dry a second time.

I scooped up the Evans as Carl dropped the Smith & Wesson. He clawed Ian's Colt from his belt and was already cocking the piece as I whirled and fired from the hip. My bullet took him square in the chest and he flew backward to land on his shoulders, then skidded a few feet farther before he stopped and never moved again.

I stood just as unmoving, the Evans clutched rock-solid in both hands, its muzzle fixed on Carl Baily's motionless form. Slowly, very slowly, as I recall, I became aware of my surroundings. I straightened like an old man getting out of his rocker, my ears ringing from the gunfire, my chest still pumping like a bellows. On legs that felt like stumps, I made my way to the bandit's side.

There wasn't much blood. I knew from hunting that when an animal is killed instantly, there usually isn't. That must have been the case with Carl, because the only clue to the cause of his death that I could see was a small dark hole in his shirt. He was definitely dead, though. You could see that in his eyes, already glazing over. Whoever said a person's eyes were the windows into his soul knew what he was talking about.

Carl Baily was the first man I ever killed, but it wasn't as traumatic as a lot of people might imagine. I'd done what I had to do in order to survive, and only a fool regrets life over death.

I spotted Ian's Colt laying in the dirt next to the dead man's knee and picked it up, then made my way back up the ridge. The gun belt lay in the middle of the trail where Carl had dropped it. I buckled it around my waist, checked the Colt's loads, then reholstered it.

You know, I just said I didn't feel guilty over my taking Carl

Baily's life, but that doesn't mean it didn't leave its mark on me. Not just the death of the outlaw, but my own close encounter with the reaper. I could still hear those bullets whizzing past my head. It makes me shudder even today to recall it.

I found Carl's horse on the opposite side of the ridge, tied behind a rock easily as big as my little shack behind Herb Smith's livery. It was a sturdy, short-coupled buckskin gelding, and a better mount than Hammerhead. There was an empty rifle scabbard under the right stirrup strap that I found intriguing, since Carl had been armed with only a revolver when he stopped me. I looked around pretty thoroughly but didn't see a long gun anywhere, so I finally decided he must have lost it . . . somewhere.

EXCERPTED FROM THE
Pocatello Democrat
AUGUST 22, 1928
"IDAHO BY-WAYS"
BY COLUMNIST
HAROLD RICKARDS

My position with this paper, as well as my association with the "Idaho By-Ways" column, which I inherited from former newsman and mentor Maxwell Tierney some years ago, has brought me in close contact with many an interesting character populating the southern reaches of our fair state, but I will freely admit that none has excited my fascination as much as my last interview, when I had the opportunity to meet with, and talk to, an aged Indian chief and former warrior of the plains called John St. Clair, previously known by the aboriginal appellation of Owl's Coup.

John, or Owl's Coup, if you don't mind (and even if you do), lives on the Shoshone Reservation north of Pocatello, having married a wonderful woman of that tribe some years back. Owl's Coup is an "elder" now, and the wisdom of his words confirms his status within his adopted tribe, but in the last century, friend Owl was a warrior of some renown among his Bannock brethren. In our rather lengthy conversation, I was able to entice this "son of nature" into relating many an intriguing tale of his exploits as a "liberator" of quality horseflesh and hunter of unparalleled skill. But it was his stories of the warpath that riveted me most firmly to my seat.

[He] tells of an encounter south of Idaho's famed City of Rocks, where he and his tribesmen encountered a "war party" of bloodthirsty "white-eyes" hot on the trail of a "good" white man who had once saved him from starvation. . . .

. . . although Owl's Coup refused to elaborate on the outcome of that battle, he did admit that he "made off" with a fine Winchester rifle to replace his old muzzle-loading firearm.

. . . while some of these bad men went on in pursuit of the good white-eye, Owl's Coup added, most ominously, to my trained ear, that "not all of them" did.

I'll leave it to the imagination of the reader to interpret the meaning of that deliberately vague response to my straight-forward question.

SESSION TEN

When one of those discs runs out, it doesn't just stop, huh? That's a pretty amazing machine, but it's distracting when it does that. I nearly jumped out of my skin that time.

Anyway, getting back to my story, I led the buckskin onto the trail and mounted. As I was leveling the reins along the horse's neck, a crow swooped in to land on a nearby rock. Its raucous caw scratched across my jangled nerves kind of like that Dictaphone just did. The scavengers were homing in on a fresh kill. I considered piling rocks over the body, since I'd done as much for the dead outlaw I came across my first day on the trail, but then dismissed the gesture as too time-consuming. I rode on without even a backward glance, and never regretted the decision. Let the carrion eaters eat, is my opinion.

I gave the buckskin my heels, and the horse settled into an easy jog. Even though I had a scabbard where I could have booted the Evans, I didn't use it. I kept the rifle across my saddlebows, in case I had to dismount in a hurry.

As I rode along, I remembered watching Carl rummage through his saddlebags for jerky back at the spring. Reaching behind me without stopping, I loosened the buckles and poked my hand inside. After a couple of minutes of fumbling, I pulled out some jerky, a few cold biscuits furry with lint, and a cloth sack half filled with sweet raisins.

Those raisins were a treat, let me tell you, but I ate the biscuits first, picking off their downy coating before popping them into my mouth like candy. I wasn't full when I quit eating, but I figured I'd better stop before I made myself sick.

The main trail continued north along the ridge, but after a couple of hours the tracks I'd followed all day veered abruptly eastward. I reined up and swung down, my heart racing as I picked my way through a tangle of boulders and sprawling conifers. With my confrontation with Carl Baily still fresh in my mind, I didn't want to risk the same mistake a second time.

It wasn't quite dark when I spotted a distant camp—just a splash of color deep within the sable hide of the forest—but the sun was down and the air was turning frosty. I could already see my breath.

Leaving the buckskin tied to a sapling well off the trail, I made my way through the rocks. Finding a spot where I would have a decent view of the camp without exposing myself in silhouette, I bellied down and eased my head past a piece of crumbling rock ledge. I saw Lucy right off, standing above a small blaze with both hands held toward its warmth. Della sat on the ground nearby with McCandles at her side, sharing a blanket draped over their shoulders like sweethearts. From that distance, probably a quarter of a mile away, I couldn't tell if Ian's wrists were still bound.

There was no sign of McCandles's gang, which worried me since they had been between us all afternoon. They had to be out there somewhere, but I couldn't see them, nor could I figure out what might be holding them back. As easily as I'd located the camp, I knew Yakima Tom and the others had to have seen it.

Remembering what Carl had said about Yakima Tom spying me back at the spring, even though I'd considered myself well-hidden at the time, I began to grow nervous. Indians seem to have a reputation for uncanny wilderness abilities, a trait I've never been able to confirm, although I was dead certain that evening that I didn't want to put it to the test. So with the light draining swiftly from the sky, I slipped back to return to where I'd left my horse.

It wasn't easy finding my way with the fading light changing all the landmarks. When I finally came to the spot where I expected to locate the buckskin, my first thought was that I'd gotten turned around. Then I noticed the peeled bark on the sapling where I'd knotted my rope, the trampled ground underneath it, and a chill that didn't have anything to do with the temperature wrapped itself around my spine from skull-base to tail bone.

Dropping to a crouch, I backed mouse-like into a crevice in the rocks, releasing the Evans' safety and wondering why the h--- I'd ever locked it on in the first place. I think that was the first time I truly understood why some men load all six chambers in their revolvers. Sometimes you just have to make a decision as to which is the more likely scenario, an accidental discharge—highly improbable with a good gun—or coming face to face with a low-life killer like Yakima Tom Candy or Jud Linderman.

I expected to see Yakima Tom and the others at any moment, but the sky turned black and the stars came out, and the little clearing where I'd left the buckskin remained undisturbed.

You might think I'd begin to relax after a while with nothing happening, but you'd be wrong. I was so wound up with fear that it's a wonder the ground around me didn't start to vibrate. I sat hunched inside that narrow crevice for quite a few hours, my eyes darting like a clock's pendulum—back and forth, never stopping. Eventually though, I began to realize that my situation now was the same as it had been so many times before. I either had to act, or curl up and die on my own and save the outlaws the trouble of finding me. I sure couldn't hunker there waiting for Christmas.

I edged out of my little hideaway, the Evans' muzzle poking out in front like a hound's sniffing nose. Nothing moved and nothing seemed out of the ordinary, so, after a couple of minutes, I stood up and took a few exploratory steps away from the rock face. I kid you not, I was expecting to hear Yakima Tom's war cry at any second. Well, I heard a cry, all right, but it wasn't his.

If you've ever heard a mountain lion's scream, especially after dark, then you know that it's a sound that can turn your knees to butter. Slamming through the forest like this one did, it's a wonder the hairs standing up on my scalp didn't dislodge my cap. Then I heard it again and realized that it wasn't a cougar I was hearing. McCandles's men had made their move on the camp, and Lucy and Della were about to pay a harsh price for their part in the affair.

I ran to the ledge where I'd first viewed the camp, but, as I craned my neck past the outcropping of stone, the danged thing exploded against the side of my face.

"I got him!" someone shouted, and I could hear heavy footsteps coming toward me in the dark.

Only thing is, he hadn't gotten me. Not like he thought. He'd come close enough to scare about ten years off the tail end of my life, years I could ill afford after climbing down from my towering look-out that morning. Rock chips stung my left ear like angry hornets, but the bullet had missed me by several inches. As soon as I was able to determine which direction my assailant was coming from, I skedaddled the opposite way.

Taking a shot in such poor light, then giving away his position so soon afterward may seem amateurish to a lot of people, but it's been my experience that bad guys are seldom as wily as they appear in movies. Of course, I've noticed that the good guys aren't much better. Maybe that's why a few years back, men like Pretty Boy Floyd and John Dillinger did so well for themselves as bank robbers—and that in an age when just about every sheriff's office in the country had its own telephone.

As for me, I kept pushing deeper into the trees. The shouting grew louder and more frantic when it was discovered that I'd slipped away. I couldn't make out what they were saying, and I didn't care. I just kept running. It was quite a while before I started to think clearly again, but it eventually dawned on me that if I didn't slow down soon I was going to get myself killed. I'd either run into one of the gang members, or I'd run off of a cliff or into a tree or something.

It was hard to make myself stop. I didn't realize until I did just how scared I'd been. My chest was heaving and my legs trembled. Staggering over to a boulder, I practically fell against it, then turned and slid down until I was sitting with my back pressed against the cool stone. It took several minutes for my panic to subside.

As my breathing slowed and the shussing of my pulse retreated from my ears, I began to take stock of my situation. I was in a low cup with trees on every side, my visibility restricted to less than twenty yards in any direction. I could see the moon peeking through the piñon limbs above me, large and bright, as autumn moons often are. The moon gave me a compass point, but not much else. I got slowly to my feet. Nothing seemed familiar, and I wondered how far I'd come in my reckless dash, and in what direction. I needed higher ground for sure, and I quickly began climbing for it.

The slope behind me was steep, the footing treacherous because of the slick dead needles from the piñons. At times I had to hang onto individual trees to pull myself up. Once on top, I could see the glow of Lucy's fire. The outlaws' fire now. It was closer than I'd anticipated, but north of me, when it had been to the east before. In my flight, I'd made a quarter circle around the camp, but hadn't put more than a few hundred yards between us.

Wanting to get closer—I couldn't tell anything from here, other than that the fire was still burning—I began circling wide to the east. I was keenly aware of Yakima Tom's presence in the forest, and wondered if this was what a deer felt when it knew it was being stalked.

The moon swung past its apex as I approached the camp. I saw or heard nothing unusual. There was the wind in the trees, and the distant yipping of a pack of coyotes on the chase. Coming to a ledge similar to the one I'd used before, I dropped to a crouch, then moved as close to its edge as I dared. I could see the camp clearly, and everyone was there. Even Yakima Tom.

Dropping to my belly, I studied the camp as best I could in the poor light. Although it was late, no one had gone to their blankets. Yakima was standing beside the fire, drinking from a tin coffee cup. The other outlaws—Ben Ryder, Jud Linderman, and Reuben Stanton—were seated back from the flames, half-concealed by the flickering shadows. McCandles lay on the ground a few feet from Yakima, his arms tied behind his back, his legs bound. I'll tell you what, that boy wasn't going anywhere.

Della and Lucy were sitting off by themselves, looking far worse for wear than they had the night before. I asked myself if the situation would have been any different if they hadn't fled in the night, and the cold, hard answer that came back was: *Yeah, I'd probably be with them, trussed up like McCandles, if not already dead.*

Even in plain sight and a good eighty yards off, Yakima Tom worried me. There was a reason the bandits hadn't retired for the night. I figured that reason had to be me.

Yakima Tom was sipping lazily at his coffee, standing with the relaxed stance of a buck deer ready to spring into action at the first hint of trouble. Then the d---edest thing occurred. After several minutes, Yakima slowly turned to face the ridge where I lay hidden, and I swear he smiled. He spoke to the others, and Ben and Jud stirred, looking around. Reuben pulled his rifle closer and levered a round into its chamber. He levered a lump into my throat, too, and I tried to flatten myself behind a pile of stones only to discover there was no more flattening left.

Walking over to the women, Yakima aimed a hard kick at Lucy's thigh. She naturally howled, and Yakima backed off and took another sip of coffee. He called out: "You come in, kid, otherwise I hurt her plenty bad!"

I tucked my face to the ground and uttered a helpless curse. The b------ knew I was out here. He felt my presence the same way I'd felt his earlier, although I doubt he was as intimidated as I'd been.

"I ain't no man blessed with patience!" Yakima shouted, his voice echoing in the cañon. "You come in now or I cut this whore's throat."

I raised my face from the dirt. Piñon needles and tiny pebbles clung to my cheek. A surge of anger boiled through me, and I brought the Evans to my shoulder. Yakima was standing too close to the women to risk shooting at him, and the others were too deep in shadow, all except McCandles, but I didn't want to kill him. Not as long as there was a feather of a chance of taking him in.

Yakima grabbed a handful of Lucy's hair and jerked it up. Tossing his coffee cup aside, he slid a skinning knife from the sheath on his hip.

"You runnin' outta time, kid."

I snugged the Evans tight, the walnut stock cool against my jaw. Lining my sights on the low blaze of the fire, I drew in a deep breath. Yakima had twisted Lucy's head so far back it's a wonder he didn't snap her neck. Her throat was exposed and vulnerable, pale like the bark of an aspen.

"Last chance!" he shouted, then put the edge of his blade

against her throat. "You give a shout now, by God, or I open her up all the way."

I squeezed the trigger. A cloud of powder smoke blotted the camp from my view, but I could hear shouting, followed by a fusillade of return fire that peppered the ground around me. I should have realized they would see my muzzle flash. Thanks to Yakima Tom, they already had a fair idea of where I was. If I'd been quicker I could have avoided the rock chips, splattering lead, and torn sod erupting on every side of me. Instead, I had to duck my head and wait it out.

As the first burst of gunfire tapered off, I scrambled back off the ledge. Maybe they saw me in a beam of moonlight, but I hadn't gone more than a few paces when the firing picked up again. Between shots, I heard Yakima bellow: "Go get him!"

Using the half-breed's instructions in much the same way a greyhound uses a starter pistol, I bolted.

Keeping low, I made my way through the piñons. The gunfire wasn't coming nearly as close now, but every once in a while I'd hear a bullet smack into a nearby tree with a sound like a logger's axe. I didn't make it very far before I came to a boulder jutting from the side of the hill. I ducked behind it, then poked my head over the top for a quick peek at the camp. No one was in sight, and I mean no one. Even McCandles had been hauled out of the light.

I took heart in the fact that Lucy wasn't to be seen. Had Yakima Tom gone ahead with his threat, I figure she would have still been there, dead.

Something else I saw that would work in my favor before I left City of Rocks was the small, white enamel coffee pot the outlaws had been using. It lay on its side near the fallen tree trunk where Reuben Stanton had been sitting, its side and most of the bottom punched out in a jagged hole. I remembered that pot. It had been sitting about a foot to the right and a little below the fire when I pulled the trigger, as if pulled off empty and allowed to cool.

Chambering a fresh round, I scanned the forest around me. The top of the ridge was no more than fifty or sixty feet away. I longed to make a run for it, to disappear over its crest and keep on going. Instead, I took a deep breath and tried to think. There were four hardcases out there somewhere. Stalking me. Waiting for me to make a mistake.

Pulling back, I turned my eyes to the sky. The stars twinkled and the moon glowed through the swaying branches. I took another deep breath. It was time to move out.

As quietly as I could, I made my way to the top of the ridge. I paused for a look back, then dropped over the far side. I needed to put as much distance between myself and the outlaws' camp as possible, and as fast as I could, but I knew I'd have to do it slowly if I wanted to avoid giving away my position. There's a line between quickly and slowly in that kind of context, kind of like a tightrope, and I'll tell you what, I was walking it that night.

I stopped again at the bottom of the ridge and dropped to one knee. A narrow meadow lay before me, empty save for its summer-cured grass and a few low shrubs that would offer poor cover. I looked around for another avenue of escape, a route that wouldn't expose my hind side to anyone watching from above, but I didn't see anything that looked promising.

So intent was I on finding another way out of there that the clack of steel on stone from behind me nearly brought me out of my skin. I was halfway to my feet before I caught myself and sank back down. There was a chokecherry bush at my side, and I slipped inside its thorny embrace like an illicit suitor. Turning slowly so that I wouldn't rattle its branches, I studied the slope behind me. I watched and listened, only vaguely aware of my finger stroking the polished crescent of the Evans' trigger. The

Colt was a solid but reassuring lump against my hip.

It was probably ten minutes before I spotted movement along the ridge top, a pair of shadows briefly skylined between two trees. I caught my breath, then held it as the men paused to talk quietly. I couldn't make out their words, but I could hear their questioning inflections as they debated my whereabouts. In another minute they were gone, and I exhaled. Then a rifle thundered from no more than forty yards away, coming at me from the base of the ridge where I had thought myself well hidden.

I grunted involuntarily at the hot burn across my side, then, reacting in my best primitive fashion, I sprinted into the meadow like a wild-eyed fool. Several more shots rang out from the top of the ridge, the bullets slamming into the ground around my feet.

The moon was bright, but even the light of a full moon makes poor illumination for shooting. Add to that the fear that was being transfused to my feet like raw fuel and you can appreciate the shooters' imperfect marksmanship.

I didn't slow down when I reached the far side of the meadow, either. I could hear shouting and cursing from behind me as I began to climb. Most of what they were saying was garbled by distance, but I did make out a few choice words. The sentence that gave me the most hope was the loudest: "Go after him, you stupid sons-of-b----es! Before he gets away!"

I'm pretty sure it was Yakima Tom who voiced that bit of inspiration, coming from high up and far away. Using the scattered piñons as hand- and footholds, I quickly scrambled to the top of the second ridge. Although I was being pursued, my youth and good heath were paying off. I knew the others were smokers and drinkers, and, although I'm doubtful of the claims that some people are making about tobacco being a cancer risk, I know for a fact it interferes with a runner's wind and stamina.

That night in City of Rocks is why I never took up either habit.

Even so, my brain was whirling by the time I reached the top. Falling to my hands and knees, I gasped for air like a leaking steam valve. I might have been in relatively good shape compared to the others, but you've got to remember that I'd started the night both physically and mentally exhausted, not to mention half starved.

The sound of gunfire tapered off—good news for me, smart thinking for them, since a bullet hadn't come close in the last fifty yards. Getting to my feet, I wobbled back to where I could peer down the slope. I saw no one, and, except for the gentle stirring of branches in the wind, nothing moved.

I stood waiting and watching, ears straining for any faint sound. Although my side ached from the bullet that had cut a furrow below my ribs, I didn't think the wound was serious. The lower portion of my shirt was sticky with blood, but it wasn't soaked, and the pain was bearable. It could wait, I decided.

I was staring at the far ridge when I saw a spark of light from beneath a tall piñon, followed by the bark of a rifle. Quick on its heels came an odd rushing sound, like a miniature wind whistling down a narrow gulch. Then something like the knuckles of God walloped me in the center of my chest and I lurched backward, the Evans leaping from my fingers. I tried to breathe but my lungs refused to work. Then the world dropped out from under me and I was plunged into an abyss as black as a bucket of tar.

Session Eleven

I came awake to the sun shining on my face, the sky so deep and blue it looked almost violet. Clouds sailed briskly overhead, high and white save for their flat gray hulls, and the treetops were being whipped back and forth in a gusting southerly breeze. The leafless branches of nearby aspens rattled like bones in a wooden box.

I stared dully at my world—all of it above me—for several minutes, then cautiously tipped my head to the side. I took the fact that it didn't fall off and tumble to the bottom of the gulch as a good sign.

With far more effort than it should have required, I sat up to have a look around. I was sitting on the side of a ridge facing south, the sun already well into late morning. Blinking against the light, I took stock of my condition. My face was scratched down one side and my chest twinged smartly with every breath. Although the wound at my side had quit bleeding, the shirt was stuck tightly to my flesh, promising more blood when I pulled it free. My pants were ripped at both knees and my cap was gone, as was my left shoe and sock. Tentatively I rolled my arms and legs, then my neck. I could tell that everything was functioning by the multitude of aches each small motion dislodged.

It took a few minutes for me to recall what had happened. Then I immediately checked my chest for a bullet hole, but all I found when I peeked down the front of my shirt was a bruise about the size of a big man's fist. There was no blood, no concaved entry wound. Yet I had been shot. I was certain of that.

Slowly I looked around. I spotted my rifle first, lying about fifteen feet away, and eased over to pick it up with the dexterity of a ninety-year-old on uneven pavement. The fore stock was a shambles, the wood splintered beyond repair, and the underside of the barrel, exposed by the torn walnut, had been dented from a powerful blow.

There's one mystery solved, I remember thinking.

The bullet from the opposite ridge had gone through my rifle first, losing most of its velocity when it struck the Evans' iron barrel before hitting my chest.

I found my shoe half buried under a pile of faded yellow aspen leaves, my sock only inches away. I pulled on both, tucking the hole where my big toe had worn through the heavy wool well under the pad of my foot. The leather lace on my shoe was broken, and, as odd as it may seem, that was the mishap that was very nearly my undoing. I sat there staring at that broken lace for the longest time, wondering what in the h--- was I doing out there. I hurt in every joint, muscle, and fiber of my being. My sinuses felt raw, my eyes dry and rusty. I was hungry and cold and bleeding and more lost than I wanted to admit, and my chances of bringing in a killer while rescuing a couple of women from a gang of cut-throats seemed about as far-fetched as putting wings on a cow and kicking it off the barn roof.

Right at that moment, all I wanted to do was find a nice thick patch of sunny grass to curl up on, and, if I died before I woke up, so much the better. At least the pain and the anguish would be gone. Sitting there with a busted rifle at my side, a practically worn-out shoe in my hand, it didn't seem like this nightmare of fear and exhaustion would ever end.

And yet, I knew I could make it do just that. I could vanquish it all with one simple act. I could put on my shoe and start walking for home. Sure, I'd be cold and hungry and more than likely blistered from heel to toe by the time I got there, but I'd be *alive,* and I didn't reckon anyone would fault me for that.

Of course, being older and a lot more cynical now than I was then, I realize I was probably wrong about folks not condemning me for giving up. By going after the McCandles gang to rescue a kidnapped girl and bring a killer to justice, I had set myself up for censure. Success might make me a champion in their eyes, one of their own to be hoisted atop the community's shoulders and paraded about as if we all shared the same common bond of courage. But to return empty-handed would have, I believe, only confirmed what they must have already been feeling in the deepest recesses of their souls—that when the call was given, only one man, and barely that in years, had stepped forward to be counted.

No, the citizens of Coalville would not have cheered my effort if I returned footsore and alone. They would have looked at me and been reminded, always, of their own communal flaws. At seventeen, I was too young to understand that men like Herb Smith, Burt Newman, and Big Ed Farmer would see my journey as anything other than an insult to their own masculinity.

I'm not so blind any more.

Not that it mattered, since, as you know, I didn't go back. What I did do was sit there staring at my shoe and feeling sorry for myself for probably twenty minutes. Then I fixed my leather lace by knotting the two loose ends together and skipping the top holes of my brogans. Taking up my battered and probably useless rifle, I got to my feet. And I wonder now: *Is there really that much difference between courage and bull-headedness?*

I went east because east was downhill and the easiest route, and because I was feeling pretty sore and shaky. Following the narrow cañon, I soon came to the same broad meadow that the two previous cañons emptied into. There, I turned north, making my way cautiously to the mouth of the cañon where the outlaws had spent the night. Crouching low behind some brush, I eyed the distant camp closely, but there was no one there. I hadn't really expected anyone.

Spotting the tracks of their horses where they'd left the cañon, I pushed on after them. The trail was easy to follow, the trampled grass of their passage like a discolored road taking me north.

As eager as I was to catch up, I had to stop often to rest. The light-headedness I'd experienced after regaining consciousness that morning never really went away, and my hunger grew steadily as the day wore on. The wind picked up and the clouds melded into a solid mass, their bellies turning from gray to black. I could smell rain in the air. Worse, I could sense a bigger change coming. At this time of year, I feared snow.

It began to drizzle late in the afternoon but I didn't stop. I turned up the collar of my coat around my neck as my breath thickened in front of me, reminding me how ill prepared I was for bad weather. I'd lost my cap in my downhill tumble, and in my melancholy after regaining consciousness I'd forgotten to look for it. I wished now that I had, but I wouldn't go back.

I trudged on doggedly with my head down, my shoulders hunched to the deepening cold. Gradually I began to forget the trail I was following, the men I sought. As my thoughts drifted, I began to stumble over small rocks and clumps of grass that I didn't seem to notice even after almost falling. I stopped once to try to vomit but nothing came up, and I recall thinking: *You've got to put something in before anything can come out.*

When I came to a fresh set of prints crossing in front of me, I stopped in confusion. There was a large meadow on my left, with gently sloping sides covered in sparse stands of timber. Granite spires marked the far end of the meadow like a row of jagged, broken teeth. At their base, nearly a quarter of a mile away, a splash of yellow caught my eye. It took me a moment to realize the honey-hued glow was a campfire, its light filtered by the rain. With a start and a curse, I lumbered back the way I'd come. There were a couple of low boulders near the mouth of the shallow cañon, and I ducked behind the largest one.

I peered around the edge of the boulder. The first thing I saw was the horses—Hammerhead, the sorrel, Carl Baily's buckskin, and Syd's palomino among them. The outlaws had built their fire in the shelter of a tilted stone pillar that must have served as both windbreak and partial roof. I stared jealously at the dancing flames. In my imagination I could smell boiling coffee and roasting meat, could hear the sizzle of dripping grease, the snap and pop of burning wood.

I let my eyes rove about. A line of conifers fingering down from the low ridge on my left seemed to offer my best bet of approaching the camp undetected, assuming no one had been posted to keep watch. I worked my way into the trees. A layer of pine needles cushioned my footfalls, although that was hardly needed with the sounds of the falling rain to mask my advance. Dropping over the top where I wouldn't be as easily seen, I lengthened my stride.

It took me roughly half an hour to reach the far end of the trees. When I did, I dropped to my belly to wiggle up the last few feet to the crest. From this new vantage point I saw what I can only describe as a stone garden, maybe four or five acres in size. I couldn't see the outlaws' fire from there, but I could smell its smoke, made pungent by the wet wood they were using. I could hear the murmur of voices, too, interrupted from time to time by the sharp cry of one of the women.

As quietly as possible, I crept from tree to tree, edging stealthily around and behind the outlaws' camp until I came to the edge of the rocks. There I stood to press my shoulders against a slab of cold granite. Up close, the stone garden looked like a maze. Some of the boulders rose thirty feet above my head; others stood no higher than my knees. Narrow, twisting paths seemed to lead deeper into the labyrinth. I chose the one that appeared to afford the best cover.

As I wound deeper into the tangle of rocks, I soon found myself circling back toward the camp from the west. I slowed as the scent of burning wood assailed my sinuses. A haze of blue smoke hung over a gap in the rocks ahead of me. The leaning stone wall I'd spotted earlier confirmed the location. Silently I crept onto a flat-topped rock that would offer me my first close-up view of the camp. What I saw turned my blood to ice.

I'd been right about the tilted stone pinnacle offering the camp a certain amount of protection from the elements. A strip of dry earth maybe thirty feet long by eight to ten feet wide ran along the base of the wall. A smoldering campfire struggled against the damp air and rain-soaked wood at the near end of the shelter. Farther along, Ben Ryder and Yakima Tom were standing over Della. Ben was buttoning his fly, while Della pulled her ripped top closed. Her limbs seemed pale but leaden in the gray light, and her chin dripped blood that she made no effort to wipe away.

Lucy sat a few feet beyond them, her matted hair clinging wetly to her skull. I saw the same dazed expression on her face as I did on Della's, and the man's shirt she wore had been torn down the front nearly to her waist. Her trousers were unbuttoned, held up by only a single striped gallus that she'd pulled over a thin shoulder.

Ian McCandles sat at the fire with his back to the women. Although his hands and legs were free, he was still unarmed, his face lop-sided from a collection of bruises. A heavy canvas sack with leather-reinforced corners sat nearby, its flap firmly buckled. Apparently the outlaws had been more persuasive than

173

I had in getting him to co-operate.

Reuben Stanton stood on the opposite side of the fire from McCandles, smoking a cigarette as he stared into the rain. I would learn later that he hadn't approved of the rape of Lucy and Della, but had backed down when Yakima Tom threatened to blow his head off. I've often wondered if I would have done any better. I'd like to think that I would, but, then, most of us like to think we're brave when we're sitting safe at home.

What I saw next caused my breath to catch in my throat. Stepping over behind Della, Yakima Tom calmly drew his revolver. I knew immediately what he had in mind. With the gold recovered, the hostages had lost their usefulness. It was time for the outlaws to move on—without the baggage of prisoners.

I could feel my pulse throbbing in my temples as I shouldered the Evans. Although I fully intended to shoot both Yakima Tom and Ben Ryder, I was smart enough to take aim at Yakima first.

Remember that coffee pot I'd blown to h--- and gone the night before? Well, so did I. It had been sitting about a foot to the right of and slightly below my intended target. I kept that in mind as I drew a bead on Yakima Tom's head. A little high and about a foot to the left.

I slid my finger over the trigger and drew in the slack. I knew I'd get only one shot at Yakima. Before I could take it, I heard the scratch of leather on stone from behind me and froze. It was just for an instant, but it was an instant too long. Fingers clamped tightly around my ankles and I was yanked off of my perch like a ten-year-old out of a hooch show tent. With a violent, mid-air twist, I was spun onto my back before I even hit the ground. Jud Linderman stood over me, sporting a grin that would have made ol' Clootie himself proud.

"Well, well, if it ain't the runt from Coalville," he said, laughing. "Kid, you have been a thorn in our britches for too d---ed long. I told Yakima last night we oughta go find you, just finish you off so we. . . ."

He leaned forward as he spoke, reaching for the front of my shirt. As he did, I kicked out instinctively. My heel struck a crushing blow to his nose and he howled and stumbled backward, both hands cupping his face. I scrambled to my feet. Ordinarily I would have skedaddled, but my skedaddling was done for that day. As Linderman dropped the bloody fingers of his right hand to the revolver holstered at his waist, I stepped forward and swung my fist with everything I had. My knuckles collided solidly with the outlaw's mouth. Blood squirted from his lips and he staggered back with a gargled cry. His knees buckled and his eyes rolled, and for a second I thought he would go all the way down. Then he caught his balance and righted himself.

My hand fell to the nickeled Colt on my hip. I'd been carrying that pistol ever since fleeing the gulch, but I had yet to draw it with an intent to kill. Today, I did. Linderman's grip on his revolver had loosened when I struck him, but he grabbed it again, his expression twisted in rage. He fired first, and from less than ten feet away, yet he missed me clean. Oh, I felt the muzzle blast, all right. Like a warm wind pressing my shirt into my stomach. But the bullet zinged past without touching flesh.

Me? I was slower by a good two seconds, but my aim was true. My bullet hit Linderman square in the solar plexus and he grunted, then side-stepped as if trying to escape the smoke-filled gap in the rocks before death could get there to claim him. Unfortunately it doesn't work that way, and he pitched to his face, dead.

I wasted even less time mourning Linderman's passing than I had Carl Baily's. Jumping onto the flat rock, I scooped up the Evans and dropped to my left knee, all in one smooth motion. I don't remember holstering the Colt, but I guess I did.

I don't know what I was expecting. That nothing had changed? That I would see Yakima Tom still standing over Della with his revolver pointed at her head, the others scattered around him like flesh and blood figures from a nativity scene? But, of course, that wasn't the case. The outlaws had vanished, and it didn't take a college professor to theorize where they'd gone or who they were after. I reckoned this time they wouldn't leave my death to chance.

No, there was no surprise in that, but what did give me a start was seeing Ian McCandles on his feet, hobbling for the horses, still saddled and standing in the rain. And as gimpy as he was, he *still* had enough gall to latch onto the gold as he fled.

I'll tell you what, that ol' boy was a thief to his core, but, in a pitying kind of way, I admired him for it.

Lucy and Della were also making a run for the horses, but McCandles must have gotten a head start, because he had the lead. He slung the canvas money bag over the horn of the palomino's saddle and mounted. I don't know what he used as a goad, but he had the palomino running before Lucy and Della even reached their mounts.

McCandles probably thought he was going to get away, what with his former gang off looking for me, but I had no intention of letting that happen. Throwing the Evans to my shoulder, and remembering to raise the sights high and to the left, I squeezed off a round from less than fifty yards away.

It was like a stick of dynamite going off in my face. The Evans was literally flung out of my hands, and my legs took off on their own, propelling me not only to my feet, but backward to the edge of the rock, then off of that into emptiness.

I fell hard, with bright flashes darting before my eyes like miniature lightning bolts. The Evans clattered down the rock after me to land across my legs. Even in my stunned condition I could see that the barrel was bulged for several inches on either side of the mangled wood where the bullet had struck it last night, along with a three-inch sliver of metal that was curved back in a fair imitation of a banana peel. And I remembered, too d---ed late for my own good, the dent in the iron that I'd noticed that morning when I examined the damaged stock.

I'd forgotten about that during my long trek through the cold rain, and my carelessness had come close to costing me dearly. I was lucky that I hadn't lost both my hands, or at the very least a few fingers, but fate can have a twisted sense of justice sometimes, and I was spared that humiliation. Getting to my feet with all the grace of a drunken sailor, I drew my Colt with a hand still slightly numb from the Evans' blown barrel and hobbled deeper into the rocks.

I wasn't harboring any illusions about what Yakima Tom and the others would do if they caught me. They might have been willing to let me go last night, rather than waste time searching for me in the dark, but they'd kill me now for sure.

Coming to a twisting path that seemed to lead away from the camp, I fell onto it and began running as best I could in my debilitated condition. I wanted to put as much distance as possible between where I was and where I wanted to be when Yakima Tom and the others reached the spot where I had been—so to speak. I knew that with all the rain and the muddy soil, it wouldn't be hard for them to track me, but I wanted to keep them guessing for as long as I could.

There was no shortage of winding routes for me to follow—that's what made it such a perfect maze—but by letting my feet take me in whatever direction they wanted to go, rather than thinking it through from a logical point of view, I soon found myself veering first north, then east again. I finally stopped when the dots flickering across my eyes like fireflies became too numerous to count. Falling against a tall boulder, I tipped my face to the rain. My throat felt as if it had been scored by broken glass as I gulped in the damp, icy air. I had no sense of where I was in relation to the outlaws' fire. Worse, I had not the slightest idea where Yakima and the others might be.

When I felt a little more confident that I wouldn't pass out, I checked the Colt. I had a dozen extra cartridges carried in loops stitched across the back of the holster, and I hurriedly refilled the cylinder. I loaded all six chambers, and wished I had more.

Keeping the revolver cocked, I moved out. The sun had set a long time ago, and the light was fading rapidly. As the ground tipped upward, the thought crossed my mind that, if I could gain the higher ground, I might be able to recover some the advantage I'd lost when Linderman pulled me off of that rock. It's funny the way a person's instinct is either to climb or go to ground and hide. I'd done both over the past few days.

I was hoping that I'd put quite a bit of distance between myself and the others in this most recent flight, but I hadn't gone fifty feet when Yakima Tom stepped into the trail ahead of me. I've got to admit that he looked as startled to see me as I was to see him. Then he flashed that wolfish grin of his and raised his revolver.

I fired from the hip, and, with my Colt already cocked, I got off the first shot. Oh, I missed him clean, no doubt about that. Those fast-draw shoot-outs you see in the movies are nine times out of ten pure fantasy. But I did make him duck, and in that split second of time I was able to throw myself to the side.

I don't know where my bullet went, but even on a diving target, Yakima was able to put a round so close to my skull that I actually heard the lead splatter into shrapnel. A small, razor-sharp piece of either rock or bullet sliced into my cheek, leaving a scar I still see in the mirror every morning.

I rolled onto my side to return fire, but Yakima had already disappeared. I could hear someone hollering behind me, asking if I'd been found or shot, but Yakima didn't reply. I didn't blame him. Staying low, I wormed into some rocks beside the trail. Another shot rang out, striking a boulder a few feet away. That brought a crooked smile to my face. That d---ed half-breed didn't know where I was, but he was trying to flush me out.

"Yakima!"

The voice came sharp as a knife's slash from no more than a dozen feet away, and I rolled onto my back rattlesnake-quick and fired from near pointblank range. My target was a pair of legs visible below a jutting stone ledge, so close I couldn't miss. Whoever it was howled in agony as his shin bone shattered. He fell back out of my range of vision, and I pushed to my feet just as Yakima Tom came into view, scrambling for the top of a tall rock that would have offered him a clear view of my hiding place.

Yakima saw me in the same instant that I saw him, and let go of the rock. He was dropping out of sight when I snapped off a round that, by all rights, should have missed by a mile. In fact, for a while, I was sure that it had. Then I heard a long, drawn-out moan from where he'd fallen, and I knew I'd hit him.

Or, I *thought* I'd hit him. Looking back on it now, I realize it could have easily been a trap. But my mind wasn't functioning at full throttle by that time, and I foolishly poked my head up high enough to have a peek.

I'd gotten him, all right. Yakima Tom lay on his back beside the tall boulder he'd been attempting to scale. I guessed he'd figured I'd be distracted by the guy I'd shot in the leg, and I suppose I was, or I wouldn't have jumped to my feet the way I did.

The front of Yakima's shirt was a sodden mess. From the regular, pencil-thin spurting of blood from the wound, I knew my bullet had severed an artery in his chest. Yakima Tom Candy's time on earth could now be measured in seconds.

I glanced behind me. Whoever I'd shot in the leg was doing his own fair share of moaning and wailing. Listening to him, I actually felt a moment's sympathy for his predicament. I didn't envy him the suffering he'd have to endure if he survived.

Remembering that there was a third man out there somewhere, I lit a shuck for the far side of the rocks. Coming over a hump in the trail, I recognized the backside of the leaning pinnacle where the outlaws had taken shelter, and headed in that direction. Even in my foggy state of mind, I was prudent enough to keep the Colt's muzzle thrust before me as I came around the sloping stone wall.

No one was there, for which I felt an immediate sense of relief. I spotted the golden lump of Syd's palomino, stretched out flat on its side. The animal's head was thrown back at an unnatural angle, and I began swearing under my breath. I hadn't yet finished when a questioning nicker interrupted my stream of profanity. Glancing at the sopping remuda hobbled nearby, I couldn't help but smile. It was Hammerhead who had spoken. The scrawny gelding was watching me, its big brown eyes standing out like polished obsidian in the dusky light.

Keenly aware of that third man—either Ben Ryder or Reuben Stanton—prowling the rocks behind me, I hurried over to the gray's side. Like the others, Hammerhead was still saddled. I yanked the cinch tight, then pulled the hobbles free and climbed on. Keeping a wary eye on the rocks, I heeled the gelding toward the fallen palomino.

It didn't take a lot of guesswork to figure out what had gone wrong. When the Evans had exploded in my hands, the shot had gone horribly wild. I spotted the bullet's wound in the palomino's neck, just in front of its withers. The spine had been severed cleanly, assuring me that the horse had died instantly and without pain, although the realization offered little comfort at the time. I think that in my mind, the palomino had become a last tie to Syd Hackett and everything he represented. Its death brought home the finality of my losses.

Spotting a clump of ragged broadcloth, I stepped down and walked over. McCandles lay in a heap, one arm curled protectively over his head. With a complete lack of remorse, I kicked him in his ribs to see if he was still breathing.

Some heroic act that was, huh?

At any rate, McCandles groaned and rolled onto his back. He was still alive, but the paleness of his features and his fever-ish appearance was cause for concern. Had I more time, I might have felt a smidgen of sympathy for him. At least as much as the piddling amount I'd wasted on the hardcase whose leg I'd shattered back in the rocks. Instead, in a voice I barely recognized, I said: "Get up."

McCandles's eyes rolled loosely in their sockets, then came to rest on me. "You," he croaked. He closed his eyes. "Go away and let me die."

"Like hell I will," I said, grabbing a handful of shirt and haul-ing him part way up. "On your feet, you son-of-a-b----. You're going to hang for what you did, even if I have to lug your rot-ting corpse back to Coalville and do it myself."

McCandles's reply was incoherent, and I could tell he wasn't faking the severity of his condition. Not this time. If we didn't get a break soon, taking him back dead might be my only recourse.

Pulling the outlaw to his feet, I led him over to the gray. He grabbed the horn without being told to do so, but then paused. Following the direction of his gaze, I saw Reuben Stanton com-ing down out of the rocks, half dragging Ben Ryder with him. Even from here, I could see the damage my bullet had done to Ryder's leg, the shine of exposed bone.

McCandles said: "Looks like you're s--- outta luck now, bub."

"No, not yet," I replied grimly. Getting my shoulder under

his butt, I heaved him into the saddle. The canvas bag containing the gold from the Boise stage lay nearby, and I hung it over the horn. Then I climbed up behind the outlaw. The gray grunted under its heavy load, and I swear it staggered some, but, when I gave it my heels, it stepped out smartly toward the far end of the meadow.

I didn't look back until we reached the broad cañon that I'd followed north all day. I kept expecting to hear a shot, or at the very least a command to stop, but no such sound came. I finally twisted around for a final look just before we dropped into the larger cañon. In the last of the light I could barely make out Reuben standing at the edge of the outlaws' camp. He was holding a rifle in both hands but hadn't raised it. I didn't draw rein, and Reuben left his rifle at waist level, watching silently as we rode out of sight.

I think the hours that followed might have been the darkest of my life. I rode in a daze of pain and exhaustion, only vaguely aware of McCandles leaning back against my chest, unconscious for much of the way. I couldn't tell you how far we went before the gray stopped on its own. I raised my head to see Lucy and Della riding out of a grove of trees. They hauled up without comment, and I slid to the ground, nearly crumbling when my legs hit the earth. Della was astride Carl Baily's buckskin, the one that I'd ridden the day before, but Lucy was still on the sorrel, still bareback. It was Della I turned to.

"I need your horse," I said.

Her response was quick and biting and not fit to be repeated. Strip away the expletives and it amounted to a single word: *No.*

I felt something snap inside of me at her words, and I started walking toward her. To this day, I'm not sure what I intended to do. Whatever it might have been, Della must have sensed the danger, for she shinnied down the far side of the buckskin like a squirrel after a nut.

Turning back to the gray, I grabbed the waistband of Mc-Candles's trousers and yanked him from the saddle. He cried out pitifully when he struck the ground, and I swear he was bawling real tears. Although I felt no triumph in that accomplishment, I was all out of sympathy.

"Get up on the buckskin," I ordered him.

"Jesus, Joe," Lucy said. She slid to the ground and she and Della went to McCandles's side, helping him first to his feet, then onto the buckskin. Cutting a saddle string from the cantle, I lashed his wrists to the horn. I was aware of the women's disapproving looks, but I was beyond caring at that point. After strapping the gold-heavy canvas bag to the cantle behind Mc-Candles, I motioned both women onto the sorrel.

"You still figure you're in charge?" Lucy challenged.

"You figure I ain't?" I fired right back, stepping into my own rig. There was a long silence, then Lucy jumped onto the sorrel's back. Della clambered up behind her, and I motioned south.

"Let's go home," I said.

SESSION TWELVE

The next few days were a fog of cold and hunger and bone-jarring exhaustion, more an effort to survive than a victorious return to civilization.

We never saw Reuben Stanton again. If he attempted to follow us out of City of Rocks, he must have lost our trail, either in the dark or because of the heavy rains. Somehow, I've always doubted that he tried. Something about my final view of the man, standing there dwarfed by the sheer size of the leaning stone wall, his rifle slack in his hands, spoke not so much of failure as acquiescence. I think he just gave up, and I couldn't really blame him. Luck had abandoned the McCandles gang. There can be no other explanation for it. How else could you explain my accomplishments against such a hardened group of men?

My only weapon in our final push for home was the Colt. There was some jerky and raisins left in the buckskin's saddlebags, but not enough to feed even one of us a decent meal. Of extra clothing and blankets, we had none.

My intention after escaping from City of Rocks was to keep on riding until the following evening. I figured that would put plenty of distance between us and Stanton, assuming he followed, but in the end we just didn't have that much oomph left to us. It was probably around midnight when we came to a swath of wind-toppled trees and stopped. Lucy and Della got a fire going with fingers so numb Della had to hold the box braced

184

against her thigh to keep it from trembling, while Lucy gripped the lucifer with fingers from both hands to strike it. Although too exhausted to recognize it at the time, I suspect we were all on a downhill slide toward hypothermia. The one thing in our favor was that it had quit raining, although none of us could remember exactly when.

After we thawed out a bit, I built a second fire so that we could stand between them, but I don't think we ever completely dried out. I know it was quite a few days after our return to Coalville before I felt warm again.

The clouds broke apart overnight, and by dawn the sky was a crisp blue in every direction. It was still bitterly cold, though. There was fresh snow on the higher peaks all around us.

We pulled out again shortly after sunup and maintained a steady walk in a southwesterly direction all day. I kept an eye out for game, but didn't see so much as a jack rabbit off in the sage. We camped that night in a shallow draw and suppered on a tiny handful of raisins apiece, the last food we'd eat for the next thirty-six hours.

It was late in the day when we finally came into sight of Coalville. We approached the town from the north, backtracking along the same trail I'd followed going out. Lucy and Della had the lead, and Lucy kicked the sorrel into a stumbling trot while still a couple of hundred yards shy of the town limits. She made a beeline for the burned-out wreckage of the Coal Palace, dismounting in the street in front of it and dropping the sorrel's reins as if the horse no longer existed. She paused in front of the charred timbers with Della at her side, then both women entered the alley next to it. I'd learn later that Adam Hoffman had set up a large tent in back in an attempt to salvage his business.

The jail was at the north end of town, just above Herb Smith's Livery. I reined toward it, but hauled up sharp when the front door flew open and a pair of goobers in dark suits stepped onto the boardwalk. My hand dropped instinctively to the nickeled Colt. Then Jim Sanders came out behind them and I allowed my fingers to drift away—a smart move, considering the occupation of the other two.

"Joey?" Jim said, taking a tentative step forward. "Good Lord! Joe, is that you?"

"It's me," I said in a raw croak. I'd been feeling light-headed off and on ever since my tumble down the side of the ridge, and a wave of vertigo struck me then. I had to grab my saddle horn to keep from pitching to the ground.

"I'll be d---ed!" one of the suited men exclaimed. "That's Ian McCandles."

I raised my head in alarm, but Jim spoke before I could do anything foolish. "It's all right, Joey . . . Joe. These are U.S. deputy marshals out of Salt Lake City. We sent for them after you left."

"We've been looking for this jasper for a long time," one of the suits said, stepping off the boardwalk to seize the buckskin's lead rope.

It took all the willpower I had not to protest as the hemp line was pulled from my fingers.

"Come on, McCandles," the deputy marshal said. He paused to take in the outlaw's hard-scrabble appearance, then looked at me. "What the h---'d you do to him . . . beat him with a club?"

"No, but I'd gladly volunteer for the job if it's open," I replied.

The lawman gave me a chary look, then led the buckskin over to the boardwalk. The two of them unloaded McCandles while I sat there watching. After they'd carried him inside, I reined toward the livery.

"Joe?" Jim said hesitantly.

I pulled up. Jim brought the buckskin over and handed me the lead rope. "You did it," he said. "I didn't think you would.

Shoot, none of us did, but you proved us wrong, by God. I'm proud of you."

A few weeks before, those simple words of praise would have meant the world to me. On that day they were just puffs of wind. I booted Hammerhead toward the livery, intending to take care of all three horses before I went over to the Hop On Inn for a meal.

So that's how it happened. That's how I brought in Ian Mc-Candles and became a 20th-Century hero. But as you can see, it's a title I'm not deserving of. Never have been, and I'll be the first to admit it. That's why I hope you'll tell the truth this time, and not doctor my words to make me into something I'm not. I want to bury that d---ed myth before I'm buried myself, because I'm afraid, if I don't, it never will die.

ADDENDUM

I'm glad you're still here, and that you've still got some room left on your machine. I feel bad about the way I walked out last night, without even a thank you for all the time you've taken to record my story. I just got to feeling overwhelmed toward the end, like I couldn't breathe or something. I needed to get away, but I appreciate it that you didn't take offense at my rudeness.

I didn't sleep much last night. I kept thinking about all the stuff I've talked about, all the memories it stirred up. A lot of them were pretty bad, especially my treatment of McCandles, but I've got to admit that I'm kind of proud of some of them. Say what you want about the lack of nobility in my methods, I did rescue Lucy and Della, and I did bring a bad man to justice.

But it also occurred to me last night that I didn't tell you the whole story. I didn't fill you in on what happened afterward. For whatever reason, it seems like that's something that never gets told, but I think it needs to be.

After taking care of the three horses, I went over to the Hop On Inn for a plate of biscuits and eggs. I vaguely remember a lot of people just staring at me while I ate, but no one asked me any questions. I was still hungry when I quit eating, but I was too tired to ask for more. I don't think I had it in me to wait while another batch of eggs was fried.

I went back to my shack behind the livery and danged near collapsed onto my cot. I only woke up once that night, and that just long enough to drag my old buffalo robe over my head, it being like an icebox in there by dawn.

It was approaching dusk again when I woke up next. I stumbled outside, then went into the livery where I found Herb Smith sitting next to a popping coal stove, enjoying a bowl of chili. He offered me the pot and I dug in like I was starving, which I reckon I was.

It was from Herb that I learned that the two deputy marshals had already departed Coalville, their prisoner chained in the back of a two-seater carriage. Herb said McCandles looked more dead than alive, but not all that much worse than I did. I guess he meant it as a joke, but I didn't see it that way.

A few weeks later, I found out the marshals had taken Mc-Candles to Salt Lake City, where they'd collected nearly $6,000 in reward money for his capture. Then they took him up to Boise City and collected another $500, plus ten percent of the recovered gold. I wrote letters to various agencies in both Idaho and Utah to protest the theft, but it never came to anything. To this day, I've not seen a dime of that reward. I did keep the Colt, though.

Della was gone before I even woke up. You might recall me mentioning a freighter by the name of Drunk Charlie, who had been shot in the hand the night McCandles's men tore up the town. Herb told me Charlie pulled out early that morning with a load of coal for Kelton, and that Della hitched a ride with him. That was the last I ever heard of her, although a lot folks speculated that she caught a train for the West Coast. Who knows, maybe she got to see San Francisco, after all.

You might expect from watching all those Western movies that me and Lucy would ride off together into the sunset, but that's not what happened at all. I saw her around town a few times after we got back, but we never spoke much beyond a *howdy* or a *how are you doing?* She left Coalville within the week, ending up in Salt Lake City where she returned to her old trade.

I heard she was killed there in a knife fight with another whore a short while later, and supposedly buried in a potter's field west of town.

I felt a certain amount of sadness when I learned of her death, but not the kind you might expect. It was more as if I'd read of a stranger's death, and mourned not the person who was lost, but the waste of a young life.

Coalville itself didn't fare much better. Check out any Idaho map newer than the turn of the century and you won't find the town listed anywhere. What happened was that the Hop Along Mine started playing out that very winter, leading to a steady decline in coal production. The whole operation was finally shut down in the summer of 1881. Oh, there were a few exploratory shafts sunk here and there in the years that followed, but nothing significant was ever found. Ten years later, I read that the main shaft had collapsed. I'm glad there weren't any miners inside when it happened.

With the Hop Along boarded up, Coalville soon withered into dust and blew away, no different than a thousand other towns and villages from that era. All that remains today are some stone foundations and the rock walls of the jail, where Ian McCandles spent a night in the autumn of 1879.

Syd Hackett hadn't died, after all, which was a huge surprise to me, considering the severity of his wounds. But Syd was a tough old bird, and he survived not only being shot, but also Burt Newman's surgery the following day. He was never the same afterward, though, and he and I were never close again. Syd was bedridden for nearly two months, and refused to see me every time I went to visit him. Then one day Herb pulled me aside to tell me that Syd had left on the morning stage for Kelton. He hadn't even said good bye.

As I feared might happen, no charges were pressed against McCandles for his part in the Coalville Raid, as the incident was then being called. Without enough evidence to convict him of the killings, they settled on charges of robbery and mayhem—whatever that means. Unfortunately for McCandles, his reputation preceded him into the courtroom, and he was found guilty on all charges. The judge sentenced him to twenty-one years in the territorial penitentiary at Boise. It was harsh punishment for the charges, but everyone knew it was as much his past crimes as the ones he was charged with that got him put away for so long.

Ian McCandles began serving his term in the spring of 1880. He was released in July of 1898, having had three years shaved off of his sentence for good behavior. I was living in Boise at the time, and went down to the prison to meet him when he got out. I took along the nickel-plated Colt, fully loaded—six beans in the wheel—but I wasn't carrying it for revenge. Time had mellowed my anger toward the old outlaw. No, I took the revolver along because I wasn't one hundred percent certain that McCandles wasn't carrying a grudge against me. That ol' boy had taught me a solid lesson about being prepared.

It all came to naught, however. McCandles was scheduled to be released on a Wednesday morning at 9:00, but by the time I got there at 8:45, he'd already been freed and put on a west-bound train for Portland, Oregon. I would read about him in the papers from time to time over the years, for he soon drifted back into his nefarious habits. When I read that he'd been killed while attempting to rob an ice cream parlor in Spokane, Washington, I wasn't really surprised, but it did bother me in a strange kind of way. It seemed an inglorious ending for a man who had once been so feared. An ice cream parlor! Imagine that.

As for me? I left Coalville for good in the spring of 1880, thoroughly disillusioned with the town and a good portion of its citizenry.

I've said I never went back to City of Rocks after getting out of there alive in the fall of 1879, but that's a lie. I did make one more visit there.

Herb Smith confiscated both the buckskin and the sorrel, claiming them against past bills. I doubt if it was legal, but I was still a kid in a lot of ways, and I believed him when he said it was. He didn't want the gray, however, and even though he'd give both me and the horse dirty looks every time I snuck some oats out of the grain bin or watered him out of a Smith-owned bucket, he never made me pay for boarding.

The next summer when the grass came up green and the snows began to melt off the high peaks, I saddled up and rode out for good. Following Syd's example, I didn't tell anyone. Not even a note, although I doubt if anyone would have cared by then. The citizens of Coalville had grown uncomfortable with my presence. I guess they could have accepted Joey Roper, the half-orphaned woods colt, but Joe Roper, the man who had not only brought in Ian McCandles, but had left a trail of dead bodies in his wake while doing it, was another matter altogether.

It turns out Lucy had told Adam Hoffman what happened out there. Hoffman had spilled it to the rest of the town.

Me and that ol' gray took our time riding back to City of Rocks. The closer we got, the more battered I felt by conflicting emotions—drawn to go, reluctant to arrive. I wasn't even sure I had the right spot until I came across the remains of Syd's palomino. Everything looked different in sunshine.

I rode up into the rocks and dismounted. The smudge of the outlaws' campfire was still there, as was the twisted skeleton of my old Evans, furred over in a layer of winter's rust. But there was no sign of a corpse, no hint whatsoever of what happened after I rode away. I'd like to think Reuben buried his partners, then took Ben Ryder somewhere warm and dry for his leg to mend, but I guess that's something I'll never know.

I hung around for several hours, wandering about and remembering how it had all been, but as darkness started to fall I got a real eerie feeling, like you get when you sense someone watching you. I'll not lie about it. My scalp was crawling, and any notion I had of spending the night was quickly forgotten.

I swung my leg over my saddle and got out of there as fast as the gray would carry me. I rode north to the Snake River, then followed that on into Boise, where I spent the next thirty-plus years of my life.

I've thought about City of Rocks a lot since my last visit, but I've never gone back. This time, I never will.

End Transcript

OBITUARY FROM THE
Pocatello Democrat
JULY 17, 1941

Joseph Sydney Roper
1862–July 16, 1941

Joseph Sydney Roper, a long-time resident of this city, passed away peacefully in his sleep yesterday afternoon after a brief battle with pneumonia. Mr. Roper was a native Idahoan, a *bona fide* old-timer, and a frequent speaker at the Idaho History Association's monthly dinners. He was the manager of the Idaho Brickworks here until his retirement in 1935, a position he had held since his arrival in Pocatello in 1912.

Mr. Roper was preceded in death by his wife, Mrs. Agnes (Conway) Roper, and two sons, Randall Joseph, of Honolulu, Territory of Hawaii, and Lawrence Roger, who was killed at the Second Battle of Marne in France during our nation's involvement in the Great War. He is survived by one daughter, Mrs. Amelia (Roper) Henderson, of San Bernardino, California, and three grandchildren, Frederick H. Henderson, Samuel J. Henderson, and Agnes Marie Henderson, all of San Bernardino.

Mr. Roper enjoyed some renown in life when, as a young man, he was instrumental in the capture of a notorious outlaw gang which had robbed a local bank of many thousands of dollars. In addition to this atrocity, the gang kidnapped one of the bank's tellers, a Miss Lucy Little, whom he aided in rescue. A true son of Idaho's "wild and woolly" frontier, Mr. Roper's exploits were featured in numerous publications around the country, yet he always humbly denied his status as a hero.

Viewing will be at the Franco Funeral Home on Cleveland Avenue tonight from 6:00 to 9:00 P.M. Mr. Roper's body will then be transported to San Bernardino, where it will be interred by his daughter at an as yet undetermined location. In lieu of flowers, Mr. Roper had requested before his death that donations be made to the Pioneer "Old Folks" Home, where he has resided the last several years.

R.I.P., Old Friend

AUTHOR'S NOTE

In order to avoid any confusion, let me state right off that *City of Rocks* is a work of fiction. So is the American Legends Collection. That said, the rest of the Works Projects mentioned at the beginning of this novel did exist, including the Folklore Project, which is where I got the inspiration for the American Legends Collection.

I love history. It's what made me want to be a writer when I was still in middle school. In my research of the 19th-Century American West, I've uncovered stories that boggled my mind. Fascinating characters and unbelievable accounts of daring and accomplishment. But the trouble with *reading* history is that it can be so damned boring. Hair-raising excitement, buried inside a muck of tedium, like flecks of gold dust in a miner's pan.

I love fiction. I love its ability to lift readers out of their chairs and plunk them down right in the middle of the action. I love the way it can illuminate a time or place, or add clarity to a historical event.

Maybe it's because I love both so well that I wrote *City of Rocks* in the style that I did. I saw it as a way to present a story in a more exciting manner, yet still give the reader a sense of reality, the feeling that he or she is hearing about the incident first-hand. My goal was to impart the same thrill I experience whenever I stumble across a gripping drama that I'd never heard of before.

I hope I accomplished that with *City of Rocks*. I will be writing other novels under the ALC umbrella, and will have a list of titles and dates of publication on my website at: www.michael zimmer.com, as they become available.

Michael Zimmer

ABOUT THE AUTHOR

Michael Zimmer grew up on a small Colorado horse ranch, and began to break and train horses for spending money while still in high school. An American history enthusiast from a very early age, he has done extensive research on the Old West. His personal library contains over 2,000 volumes covering that area west of the Mississippi from the late 1700s to the early decades of the 20th Century. In addition to perusing first-hand accounts from the period, Zimmer is also a firm believer in field interpretation. He's made it a point to master many of the skills used by our forefathers, and can start a campfire with flint and steel, gather, prepare, and survive on natural foods found in the wilderness, and has built and slept in shelters as diverse as bark lodges and snow caves. He owns and shoots a number of Old West firearms, and has done horseback treks using 19th-Century tack, gear, and guidelines. Zimmer is the author of eight Western novels, and his work has been praised by *Library Journal* and *Booklist,* as well as other Western writers. Jory Sherman, author of *Grass Kingdom,* writes: "He [Zimmer] takes you back in time to an exciting era in U.S. history so vividly that the reader will feel as if he has been over the old trails, trapped the shining streams, and gazed in wonder at the awesome grandeur of the Rocky Mountains. Here is a writer to welcome into the ranks of the very best novelists of today or anytime in the history of literature." And Richard Wheeler, author of *Goldfield,* has said of Zimmer's fourth novel, *Fandango* (1996): "One of the best mountain man novels ever written." Zimmer lives in Utah with his wife, Vanessa, and two dogs. His website is www.michael-zimmer.com. His next Five Star Western will be *Beneath a Hunter's Moon.*